ARNITA R. LEONARD

Amethyst in Love

UNCERTAIN IN LOVE & FAITH

Printed in the United States of America.

ISBN: 979-8-9923146-6-3

Publishing: Nita Nae's Books © 2015

Imprint: (Amazon.com, 2019 eBook/ Print 2025)

*** Character P.O.V. (point of view)

AVAILABLE & COMPLETE

Apocalyptic 7 – Salvations Cry (Lulu, 2025)

Unconditional Counsel (CFP, 2020, Rev. Lulu, 2025)

The Ghosts of Slavery's Dance (Lulu, 2025)

Mercy Undercover: A Det. Brenda Sayers Story (Lulu, 2025)

Embrace the Dawn to Live Again (KDP, 2024)

FUTURE BOOKS (WIP's)

Unconditional Counsel 2 — Fate Unbroken!

Apocalyptic 12 — Angels of Heaven's Armies

The Container

Opposing Fruit

The Heart of an Untold Legacy: A Father's Story

ACKNOWLEDGEMENTS

I give all honor to God, who gave me the desire to write, not that I may be good at it, but I enjoy writing to the fullest. I love using my imagination to bring characters to life and see the manifestation of what God gives me during the process.

I owe HIM everything — that's it and that's all.

INTRODUCTION

AMETHYST IN LOVE was my first short love story that tells of a time when your upbringing doesn't always give you the tools to navigate life. When love you are supposed to receive lacks heartfelt sincerity. Enjoy this short read!

PROLOGUE

AMETHYST IS JACQUELINE'S favorite color. Crystalline quartz in shades of purple, lilac or mauve, a stone traditionally worn to safeguard against drunkenness and to instill a sober mind. Amethyst comes from the Greek meaning 'without drunkenness,' and they believed the amethyst protects one from contamination. If anything, this allows one to keep a sober mind about life. Amethyst symbolizes piety, humility, sincerity, and divine wisdom. Spiritual understanding is something we should pursue from the Holy Spirit, and not from the world.

A corrupt history dooms the future unless God's plan is for you to learn from your history. God revealed in His Word that people perish for a lack of knowledge. Wisdom in how to use that intelligence is what's lacking these days—Common Sense. We will never advance to fight for a stronger existence and a better state of seeing if we continue moving in the same circle. We end up looking at our former selves and remain stuck where we are—Arrested Development.

Jacqueline grew up with misguided thinking, as her parents did not subscribe to any religion or even atheism—the view not to believe. Jacqueline lived a pristine and sheltered existence. The generation of we don't teach or talk about such things as chastity or what it means to love someone was her burden of being born into this family. It was taboo, and although her parents respected each other in their own fashion, they elected not to love their children as proper parents should—whether boy or girl. There is never an excuse to disregard your child.

JACQUELINE'S MONOLOGUE

I GREW UP NOT LEARNING what genuine love was. Wanting but never understanding how to seek it out or even knew what to look for if it ever manifested itself in my life. Never looking at what I craved for my heart. I didn't have any positive and long-lasting examples. Financial stability, well, my father took care of that. I was to go to college, get a suitor, become married, have offspring, and continue happily forever after—as my mom instructed me, because that's all she knew and that's what my father expected of a girl child.

After my parents died, being lost was an understatement. My life didn't turn out along the path they required. My destiny was to do and be something different. The genuine love around me. I didn't understand how to receive or maintain it, but my wanting kept me on the path of seeking. I had to break the cycle and discover what was missing. What did I know about love or faith?

They never discussed God in our home. It was taboo, and none of the three kids dared to speak of any god. They didn't allow discussion of even mythical gods—no Zeus, Superman, or Thor. So, what's a young woman to do? Live out the course before me. Later, to find myself in a place of wanting, bare and devoid inside. For what was I searching? What is authentic love, anyway? What did marriage represent other than the robot existence seen from my parents?

CONTENTS

Chapter 1

Unwanted Existence

AT THE AGE OF 11, my mother had given me the hard truth. Something a child should never hear from a parent or anyone. My mother tried to protect my innocence. She could care-less about my mental well-being, as she too had lost the love of my father to his work.

"Baby, I love you, but I was never one to nurture or know what it was to be a good parent," she says.

Me, unable to comprehend, "Why doesn't he love me, momma?" I ask. I guess, because she talked and simulated love in her own way, I didn't ask the same of her.

Sighing, as if she didn't want to answer but had to, "Your father never cared for a girl child. Never did he have any use for you. It was the boy heirs he needed, and I gave him two."

This conversation was something I read in a book somewhere — Cinderella. It wasn't supposed to happen in real life. In our country, parents took care of their children to the best of their ability and did not leave them to fend for themselves like the children left to their own devices in Peter Pan. We were living in America. As a girl, I was nothing, and I was stuck in this impossible life. Stuck being raised by parents who... never mind. You understand what they were. Conditions of their own upbringing.

"So, because I'm a girl, he has no room in his heart for me?" I understood that much. It was a heart situation.

"I'm afraid not, Jacqueline." Grabbing me by the shoulders. That was as close to a hug that I would ever receive from my parents. Even on their deathbeds.

"How could you love a man like that, momma?" I was ashamed because I could see that it was their choice. I hadn't seen it in other families. So, I knew the difference.

"Our marriage was an arranged one by our parents, but I fell in love with your father before I knew who he was inside. When I gave him sons, he was happy, and he showed love toward me. When you came, he left out the room and only came to visit me when I got out the hospital. I cannot put all the blame on him. I know his parents had a hand in what he was to become."

My parents did not belong to any culture where arranged marriages were common. This story seemed to be an excuse for her to blame her history. My mother told me that my father was half German and half African. His family was wealthy. It was all about the money for them. He had to marry someone worthy enough for his lineage. My mother's family was wealthy, too.

Her barren attempt to comfort me with her stare did nothing to ease the pain in my ears or heart. Was I supposed to feel just as sorry for her as I did for myself at eleven?

"A man like him. I could never marry him. I hate him and I hate you!"

"Sometimes we don't always get to choose. I'm so sorry."

That day, I grew up faster than my mind could plan my reality. Ultimately, I felt pity for my mother, and for the women my brothers would marry someday. My father made sure they emulated everything he was. My existence as a human being was such a burden to my whole family that my mother, unbeknownst to my father, made sure she could have no other children. I never asked to be here. 'Why hadn't they just given me away,' I thought.

~

The stereo playing my favorite song, I consciously move to the beat, looking out into the street. My very existence wanted love, but I didn't want to seem like I was desperately seeking for it. Nahiry always pushed me to date somebody. She didn't want me to be lonely. Not having someone in my life wasn't the only problem within. She always meant well. She did not know what it meant not to have a family to love you. I wanted no one to experience what I did as a child.

"You know you're about to hit twenty-nine? What are you waiting for?" Nahiry asks.

"Wow!" That statement hit deep. Reality check. What was I waiting for?

"I didn't mean to make you feel bad. It's just a question."

Then, that old proverbial biological clock, in which society is good for making you feel inadequate about taking your time to find the right one for you. Also, it didn't help I romanticized about every man in the books I read.

It was a bright day. The moderate breeze was warm enough to sit outside and not burn. The trees were barely moving at the tops of the arrow-tipped branches, but it was enough to be thankful for. My sigh of the mundane told the story as I opened the French-doors to step onto the mahogany stained deck. Drawing in a deep breath of fresh air. Sitting at the lounge table, I was looking at the back cover of a paperback I had completed reading. I adored romance novels, more than any other. Putting myself inside the story to escape what I knew only to be in books. Lonely in thought and life, I could only acknowledge that I would repeat the story my parents had taught me. To either be alone or marry for other than love.

~

At thirteen, waiting for swimming practice. The school bully had been picking on one of my friends and I would not take her bullying lying down. I stepped in front of her and punched her. She ran to the nurse's office because of a bloody nose and snitched. My mother was called, and so was my father, but he never came. Although I didn't get suspended that day, my mother was anxious and tried to send me to my grandmothers for the evening. My grandmother Ruthy was unavailable to save me, as my mother put it. I didn't know or understand why she would want to send me to my grandmother's. What had I done was so bad? My mother fed me earlier than my brothers and made me stay in my room. I knew my father was stern. I saw him give a good talking to, to my brothers, and that was that. If I had the chance to explain, then my father would understand why I did what I did. I was protecting my friend. Isn't that what friends do?

My father came into my room after eating his supper. He never said a word, but I remember the belt in his hand: mahogany brown, thick and wide. I think for that exact moment in time, my consciousness was not there. I had escaped the reflection of my father thrashing me for standing up for what was right. This was the day that turned my understanding of fairness upside down. Not only was I not loved by my father, but now fairness was out the window as well. What was love, anyway? It was the first and last day my mother told me the truth, again. "Your father never wanted a girl, child."

~

"If only I could be that particular." My imagination often ran wild with flights of fancy. If only I could be glamorous and in love. I glared into la-la-land once again at the face on the book for a few seconds. "Only in your dreams, Jacqueline. Only in your dreams."

I grabbed the volume off the table, deciding I would rather daydream in the house. I didn't want to be bothered by any of my neighbors.

"Hi, Ms. Abner!" She waved back to say hello. I went into the house, immediately feeling sorry for myself—which was often.

Later that evening, the phone rang, and I knew who it was as I glanced at the clock. My neurotic friend called me every day at the same hour.

"Nahiry, what's going on?"

"How did you know it was me?"

"Why wouldn't I? You call every day at six on the dot, and we go through the same routine."

"Am I that predictable, or are you having a bad day?"

"Only when you call me. I even know when you're calling Jerry. How is my buddy?" Silence. I had realized in that moment, maybe I was having a bad day or something else was going on with her. "Oh, you two must not be speaking much these days. You never told me what you did last night."

"I guess I am predictable if you can guess over the phone."

"Nahiry, I've known you for fifteen plus years, and you always call at the same time because you've been at the same job for nine of those years. When you come home, you want the latest gossip from everybody, and you start with me only because I'm your best friend, and you know you won't get too much out of me because my existence is boring and nothing exciting ever happens to me. But I appreciate you."

"Stop it, Jackie, you're bringing me to tears. You know you need to stop."

Figuring I'd better get off the subject of Jerry. It seemed like Nahiry's love story was even more of a touchy subject than my own.

"So, have you talked to Sharon yet? I wonder if she's ready to drop baby Christian yet?"

"No, I have not. I'll call her after I hang up with you."

After a half an hour, I knew I had better cut this phone conversation shorter than usual. "Okay, Nahiry. Call me if you hear anything." Turning on the television, I saw the novel I had just read was on that week's best-sellers list. Remembering the passion the lover had for her companion. My thoughts roamed over whether I would ever find happiness and the right man to love me completely. Would I even know if someone genuinely loved me? I knew that sometimes men you perceive to want so badly may not meet your expectations.

The next morning, walking into work, I said hello to Bubba, the security guard in the lobby of the medical building. I walked down the hall to the office, never failing to display a big smile every day. Into the office I went, "Good Morning Cynthia."

"Good morning, Jackie."

My daily routine, to say hello to Cynthia, put all my things away in my office and head to Dr. Simmons' office. "Good morning, Dr. Simmons," I says.

"How are you this morning, Jacqueline?" He stands to greet me.

"Fine. How are you?"

He sighs, as if he had something pressing on his mind. "As good as expected."

I worked as his RN for five years. Being a constant professional in and out of the office. I would always keep my relationship with the staff a professional one. Even though Dr. Simmons made attempts before, he had since come to his senses and didn't ask anymore. He never married, and I could only assume that it was because of his dedication to his practice. Although, there was no shortage of woman he would date. His status as a bachelor, physician, with no offspring, handsome looks, and absence of ex-wives made any woman inclined to seek his attention. Time after time, the women were only out for his money. Sometimes, he would bring his dates in order to see what I thought. He would leave them in his room saying, "Enquiring minds want to know." He often says he would never get married or have any kids. I knew better, as his eyes lit up when children came into his office. His care for kids was more than a mother could ask for in a father figure. His first name was John, but I never called him that. I kept my admiration of him to myself. That was the same with all men I was fond of, and he was no exception to the rule.

It was the lunch hour, and Cynthia normally ordered for everyone. "Cynthia, what are you going to order for us today?"

"Now, Jackie, you know the place. Tell me what you want."

"I know," pointing to the picture on the menu. "I just thought I would annoy you today—even though I never annoy you... other than today."

"Jackie, I want you to know you are the weirdest person I have ever met, and yet I like you. You are who God made you to be, and you never try to be something you're not. Being an only child, I wish you had been my sister."

I was so touched, so I went to hug her, just as Dr. Simmons came out and he says, "Can I get a hug too?" Everyone laughed, and Cynthia ordered our food.

Following Dr. Simmons into his office, I closed the door behind us.

"Yes? Can I do something for you, Jackie?"

"D...Dr. Simmons, do you think I'm weird?"

His slow response was telling as he sat in his chair. His glance was curiosity toward my question, but he answers, "Are you asking whether you are unique in how you carry yourself, then yes, but if you are talking about being creepy, standoffish, then no — unless it comes to me — or is it, all men?"

I cringed, because maybe he was right in his analysis. "Okay, but about your analysis." He knew I needed more.

"For the past five years, I have made a pass toward you four or five times, and I haven't gotten a response from you. Not even...why are you harassing me? You haven't responded to any of it. You act as if you were raised by nuns or prefer the same sex."

Apparently, he had been wanting to say that to me for a long time. His shoulders relaxed when he finished. I didn't know how to explain, but whether I liked men or the opposite sex needed clarification. But it was almost as if there was nothing holding me back. I talked about my past, and to my amazement, it turned out extremely well.

"I am attracted to men only, but it's also because I respect you a lot, and I don't feel I should be less than respectful and professional toward women or men who I admire."

"Why do you admire me so much?" His eyes locked on to mine.

"I see the way you are with children, even though you have none of your own. My father had no feelings for children, especially for his daughter. Sons were okay, but daughters were for their mothers only. I grew up with a father who only talked to me if I did something wrong in school or when I needed discipline. Discipline was my father's and his alone. My mother tried to shelter me from his lack of interest. Most daughters are daddy's little girls, but I was not a little girl to anyone. My mother loved me in her own way when my father wasn't around, but I didn't receive tenderness or affection in my home." In that moment, I realized I had not shared my past with anyone other than Nahiry. He sat back, and I continued. "I love children—that's one reason I took this position. My father made sure we wouldn't want for anything financially but emotionally; he just didn't want me. I try my best to be open and honest, but to love someone, I don't know what that is like. When he died, my mother didn't want to live anymore. She loved him more than she loved us or herself. At least, she didn't love us equally or try to show it in front of my father." The sarcasm revealed the bitterness I still held inside. "She protected me from everything because she knew she would die soon after he did. She died of a broken heart, and none of her children could fill the void left by my father's death. Another reason I wanted to work here was when you walked me around the office, your passion for kids was clear. I saw how you treated them. You leave me speechless. I knew you were the man to work for. I still see the depth in your eyes when a child comes into your office. Money isn't the reason you do what you do, and it's not mine either."

His smile revealed pleasure from my words. Standing and stretching his upper torso, "I'm glad you think of me that way. It's appreciated. I, like you, didn't grow up without, but believe me, I am no saint, and I don't plan to be one."

I chuckle. "If my father would have given me a fraction of the attention you give to these kids, I wouldn't be such a weirdo, I guess." Jovial in the moment of sharing my life story, reality sank in. I shared my dark secret about my family with John. I didn't know how to face him after leaving his office. When I came back into the office to let him know a patient was ready for a check-up, my admiration for him was back intact. "Okay, I'll be there in a minute," he says.

He lit up the room, as he said hello to the little girl who was sitting on the examining table. Amy smiled as she jumped up to give him a hug. "Oh! My, what was that for?" She jumped back up on the table. "I know you're my doctor, and I don't want you to forget me when I get big." Her expression changed as fast as snapping your fingers. "I am here to get these stupid shots for school," she says.

"Oh! That's right, you're moving away." Her somber look says she wanted to cry. At only six, she was very aware of everything.

"Dr. Simmons, will I ever see you again?"

"I am sure of it, because you know why?"

She crosses her arms in frustration. "Why?"

"Before you leave, I will give you an autographed picture of Ms. Jacqueline and me from the office, and I will ask Cynthia to give you, my address. So, when you move to Washington, you can send me a picture of yourself every year as you age, and I also want you to send me a letter updating me on how you are doing and if you are feeling well. Is that okay with you?"

"Sure, Dr. Simmons." She looks toward the floor.

"I will miss you a lot too, Amy." When he finished with Amy, we both walk into the hall and I get the vaccinations to complete Amy's day.

"I told you, Dr. Simmons." He just laughs as he headed to his office.

After the last check-up, everyone stayed an extra hour to clean up and catch up on all the paperwork. It was Friday, and no one had any plans except for Dr. Simmons. He was heading to a party for one of his colleague's wife's 40th birthday.

"Have a wonderful time, Dr. Simmons." Cynthia smiles his way.

"Thank you, Cynthia, and don't work too late."

"I won't. You don't pay me enough to stay too late." They both laugh as he headed to the elevator.

I was curious how he would act toward me now that he knew parts of my past. I didn't want him to see the questioning in my eyes. "Goodnight, Dr. Simmons." His voice soft to my ear, "Goodnight, Jacqueline."

Dr. Simmons was gone, so I moved my attention toward Cynthia. "Cynthia, would you like to have dinner?"

"I would like to, but I have to meet my boyfriend at his job. I'm sorry. Raincheck?"

"You don't need to be sorry. I don't blame you for going to see that hunk of yours. If I had a man to spend my time with, I would have been out of here at five o'clock on the dot. Don't worry about it, I understand. And, yes, you can have a raincheck."

"Someday you will find the right man for you. God will send him. You never know, he may be right under your nose."

"I hope so, Cynthia. I've been waiting for the one all my life, and I'm not getting any younger."

"Let me give you some advice. Open your heart to experience everything, try almost anything once within reason, and don't give up your dreams if you haven't already. The bible says, *'He that finds a wife, finds a good thing and favor with the Lord.'* I've never asked before, but do you have a faith preference?"

It was confession day for me. "You know, Cynthia, I didn't grow up believing in any god. My family never mentioned God or faith in our house. Other kids in my school would talk about it, but my family didn't allow discussions about God or faith in our house. I would try anything if I thought it might bring the man of my dreams to life, and he falls deeply in love with me. I hope it happens before I turn thirty."

My birthday was still months away, but I'd been counting down every year, month, and day in the build-up to me turning thirty. Thirty for me was a pinnacle turning point for me. Most of the women in my family were married way before then.

"I wouldn't want you to turn to God just to get a man, but the man upstairs tells us to plant the seed and He will give the increase. I will pray for you. Speaking of age, when were you born, Jackie, if you don't mind my asking?"

"I was born on the 21st of February." My willingness to reveal my age seemed to surprise Cynthia.

"You're twenty-eight, and still full of life. You have time. I'm sure God has a plan for your life too, Jackie." Her advice seemed genuine, and I took it to heart. The things she was saying were foreign to me. I didn't discount them to be true or not. I just didn't know how to process them.

"How in the world did you get to be so wise?"

"I grew up in a single-parent family and my mother taught me never to give up on my dreams. I never ever take life or the people I love for granted. My faith in Jesus Christ has kept me strong and grounded."

Seeing so clearly the love Cynthia had for her mother. She spoke with an elegance that I couldn't speak about on my own.

"Your mother is obviously a wise woman. I see she brought you up with love and dignity. That's admirable in you.

"I could say the same about you."

Why would anybody admire me? I had to ask, "But why would you admire me?"

"I see you every day with a smile on your face—even though you may not feel so great. Someone else might not notice, but I know when you're preoccupied with something outside of work."

My body shifted with relief again.

"And you still have your cheerful face on in front of the children that come in here. Even when you're down, you generate warmth and love toward them, and you do the same for Dr. Simmons. It's in your nature, Jackie. God gave that to you in your DNA. You were born with it—a natural encourager."

"Oh! Come on." My cheeks were in a warm flutter. Cynthia saw something that I didn't see or recognize in myself.

"To tell you the truth, you and he are very much alike. The pay is not that great, but I wouldn't leave this job for anything—as long as the both of you are still working together. You both have always treated me with respect, and I appreciate that very much. My last job was demanding, and I didn't mind that part, but they treated me as though I wasn't even a person. Just someone to be at their disposal. I enjoy coming to work here, and few people can say that and mean it about their job."

The conversation ended. We both headed out for our destinations. Cynthia to her beloved, and me to my empty abode, as always. Walking to my car, I recalled the conversation I had with John and wondered if it was a mistake. There was nothing I could do about it now.

I stopped at my favorite deli and picked up a sandwich for dinner.

Chapter 2

The Bowling Connection

SATURDAY MORNING, after talking to Cynthia last night, I woke up with a sense of newness. My expectations for the day weren't any different from any other, but my mind clung to the fact that it was up to the heavens to send me someone to love or not. Living a life with no financial worries would be anyone's dream come true. Unfortunately, it's a lonely existence, even when there are those around me who fulfill a smidgen of void in my existence. I had the money my father left me through my mother, a house to live in and a job that I cherished every day, but I wasn't complete. I'm not talking about the cliché of having a man to complete me. To share a life with someone who didn't make me feel like I was less than. To understand the nature of a loving experience.

Heading over to Nahiry's' house, it was bowling and then lunch every Saturday morning. I figured I'd call first, like she did every Saturday, to shake up things.

"Hello, Jackie."

"How did you know it was me?" We both laugh.

"I am on my way out of the door right now. Not sure if you and Jerry have patched up your spat, I didn't want to come and catch you two in the sack."

"Now you know better. No one sleeps over here unless they put a ring on my finger."

Unfortunately, I knew otherwise from her previous relationship. "Nahiry, you let Kenny move in with you, and he didn't put a ring on it."

"I was in love with Kenny, and we talked about getting married. That was the only time I have ever let anyone sleep here. Anyway, you don't have to pick me up. I need to stop at the store. I'm closer, so I'll just meet you there."

~

Riding down Western, I soon arrived at 30 Lanes Bowling Alley. Nahiry was already waiting out front for me. We smile, and I parked. Reaching Nahiry at the doors to go in, she was cheeky.

"What lane did we get?" I ask.

"Lane 29."

"I guess that's okay!" But I started smiling with great exaggeration. She thought something was wrong with me.

"Anything wrong Jackie? What's going on with you?"

I didn't figure on getting that type of response. "No! Do you notice anything different about my outfit?"

"No. What are you talking about?" she asks.

"Just look." After a minute, I opened my bowling bag.

"You got a new bowling ball and bag!"

"Yes. They got my favorite color, and you know I had to get shoes to match."

"You kill me. I don't see you for a week, and you come back looking better than I do. But you know even though you have a new ball, it doesn't mean you will win." Nahiry was now playful.

"Why, I usually win anyway?"

"You are only up by three games. You never know what might happen. I just might catch up to you," Nahiry says, though she didn't sound too confident.

"You might. I haven't tried out this ball yet, so let's play."

The clerk greeted us as usual, and we head down to the lane and set it up to bowl.

"Do you want to go first?" Nahiry says smiling.

"I'll let you go first this time, since we have company. I'll cheer you on."

Nahiry and the guy next to us were flirting. She was trying to be cute and rolled a one-pin drop, and he came over to give her some advice, which is exactly how she got Jerry. I knew her play.

"What's your name?" he asks.

"Nahiry. What's yours?"

"John, nice to meet you, Nahiry."

"Hi, John. How long have you been coming here?"

"Not too often. I bowl to hang out with my brother. He's the better bowler out of the both of us. How often do you come here?"

"We come here together every Saturday. John, this is my friend, Jackie."

"Jackie and Nahiry, this is my brother Craig." He came over to shake our hands.

"It is great to meet you, ladies." Craig says.

Craig turned around to take his turn at bowling. Laughing under my breath because after our long friendship, I still couldn't believe how fast Nahiry could pick up a guy. I was polite, but not interested in making lengthy conversation, so I too went up to bowl. I figured I'd play the game with a little less grace than Nahiry did. "Go, Jackie, go!" I looked back at Nahiry to find her and both men watching. As I was about to bowl, I thought, why not make this day interesting. I rolled a gutter ball. Nahiry looked as if to say, *'why would she roll a gutter ball and then roll a five-pin drop?'*

As I walked back to sit down, Nahiry looked at me with a devious expression. "It's your turn to turn up the heat, Nahiry." Giving her the side eye. I sit next to Craig at the score table, looking ahead down the alley. Craig was a typical ego maniac, and I knew I could get his goat. First impressions are everything, and he carried himself as arrogant. If there was one gift, I knew I had, I could scope out a personality as soon as they opened their mouths. He carried himself like a clown, although his brother John seemed the opposite, and that was in just the first ten minutes of meeting.

"So, how long have you girls been coming here?" Craig asks.

"Oh! About two years."

"You mean you've been coming here every Saturday for two years?"

"Yes! Why so surprised?"

"But you rolled a gutter ball, and you only knocked down five pins."

"So, I bowl for fun—not competition."

"Oh! Okay! I get it."

"And what do you get?"

"You just come here to pick up guys."

My body turns toward his. "What kind of nonsense is that? You don't even know us. Looking for guys is the last thing I want to do when I come here. I come here to bowl and have an enjoyable time with my friend. Just because I bowl the way I do, doesn't mean I'm here to pick up douche bags. So, next time you meet two gorgeous women, don't just assume they're trying to troll. And anyway, I can beat you at bowling any day."

"Not likely, honey." Now his smugness went to another level.

"Well, since you think you can beat us *girls*, let's make a wager. You better ask your brother before you commit to losing, though."

"Hey, John! Jackie over here has bet us that these two girls can beat us two out of three." His confident tone was disturbing.

"Oh! Is that so?" John says.

"Jackie, what's going on?" Nahiry asks, coming back from bowling her turn.

"Craig here was kind enough to put us in our place, and I bet him we could beat them two out of three."

"Really?" Nahiry says.

"Really!" I confirmed.

"I guess then we will make a bet where we don't lose too much." We turn to the one and a half men and make the wager.

"Well, if we win, you get to pay for three games each for the both of us," Nahiry expressed joyously.

"And what do we get if we win?" Craig asks, smiling large and clearly dimwitted.

"You pick." I tell them.

Before Craig could open his mouth, "Okay! If we win, then you have to take us out to dinner tonight." John says.

I responded kindly, "That's simple enough. If you don't ask for sex, we're ready." Sarcastically. "We aren't that easy, you know. We do at least have to wait for a second date." I glance straight at Craig, knowing it would get under his skin even more. He was gorgeous, I give him that, but I knew he was used to women falling all over him.

Nahiry smiles confidently and says, "But who says you will even get the dinner!"

After that minor exchange, Craig and Nahiry went to pay for an extra game and continued to exchange pleasantries. "Don't worry, you will take us to dinner." Craig says.

We finished our previous game and set up to bowl against each other. I went first and bowled a strike.

"Oh, how lucky can you get?" Craig remarked.

Nahiry went next. Another strike and then neither of the men could pick up a strike. "The scores are as follows," I say, smiling as the first game concluded, "John 153, Craig 140, Nahiry 162, and Jackie 210."

Craig and John huddle on one side of the lane and then they both turn towards us. "John, I think we've been cheated. How come you girls rolled a gutter ball when you first came?" Craig waited for an answer from either of us, as he folded his arms.

"We always do it to make sure the lane works." I explain.

"You mean you do that every time you bowl?" John asks.

"Well, one of us does. We alternate turns. See, I thought I would pick up a game from you gentlemen to make it interesting, but there was a serious challenge from Craig."

"She set us up, John." Craig felt perturbed.

"And you were in on this also, Nahiry?" John asks.

"No, I did not know what she was up to. I just went along because I know how she is." Which wasn't true.

"Well, I think the bet is off," Craig says sullenly.

"Oh, no! We won this game fair and square. No one told you to assume we were twits. You, my dear Craig, should not assume we come to bowl to pick up guys." With a dumb look on his face, he agreed to pay out on the bet. "I figured this would also be a good lesson for you to learn."

John turned to Craig. "You said that to her?" John cries out, shaking his head.

"So, what time next week shall we come and collect on our debt of our free bowling games?" I ask.

"I guess about the same time?" John says, smiling at all that just happened.

Nahiry motioned to me to step to the side so we could talk. "Let me talk to you for a second."

"What is it, Nahiry? I know you have something up your sleeve."

"Why don't we take them out to dinner, anyway? We did kind of trick them too."

"Out of the question. He deserves what he got." I was now crossing my arms and huffing. Why should he be rewarded for being a jerk?

"Jackie, I like John, and I want to get to know him."

"So why don't you take him out yourself, Nahiry? I'd rather go on a blind date than be at the same restaurant with Craig."

"I don't want to go out alone with him. Please, Jackie, come out with me."

Because I hesitated a bit, Nahiry knew I would give in. "Okay! If Craig gets any ideas, though, it won't be my fault if I have to break something." As Nahiry was the only one who knew Jackie was a black belt in Tae Kwon Do.

"Okay! I'll talk to them and see what they say." Nahiry was excited. She walked over to the two men, who were both awkwardly waiting around now to play their other games.

Nahiry's smile matched John's eagerness to hear what she had to say. "We figured since we did kind of deceive you a little, we would take you out to dinner tonight, anyway."

Immediately Craig states, "Oh! Well, no, thank you. We'll just pay on our debt next week."

"See, I told you, Nahiry." Craig was a jerk. I didn't want to go out with them, anyway. I was doing this for Nahiry.

John pulls Craig over to the side. "What are you doing, man?"

"What do you mean, what am I doing?" Craig replies.

"I like Nahiry, and I want to get to know her, and I don't think she will go out with me without

Jackie." I couldn't see his face clearly, but I could hear John pulling the big brother card. "You owe me one, Craig, and I wouldn't ask you if I didn't think you would at least have a civilized time. And you are getting a free dinner. Now, why would you pass up on that opportunity?"

"I guess it is too good to pass up." Reluctantly giving in to his brother's request.

"And besides, Craig, Jackie is a beautiful woman."

"Well, she looks all right."

"She looks more than all right, and Nahiry's hot, too. So at least be civil and try to get along with her."

"Okay! But I don't have to like her," Craig grumbled.

"All right. Just let me do all the talking." John says.

"Ladies, we accept your gracious offer and would love for you to take us to dinner."

"What time shall we pick you up?" Nahiry asks.

"Six-thirty would be fine." John says.

"And where shall we pick you up from?"

"You can meet us at my house if that is, okay? I'll give you the address." Handing her the information, "Thank you and see you ladies at six-thirty."

By the time we all finished, it was noon, and we headed out to our cars after eating lunch in the bowling alley.

"So, what do you think of him?" Nahiry asks.

"He's arrogant, snotty, and a real jerk."

"I wasn't talking about Craig." We both laughs. "John, I mean."

"I know. I just had to get that off my chest."

"So, what do you think of him?"

"I'll tell you one thing, those two are polar opposites, and John is perfect for you. He seems like a real man. Now, let's see how long it lasts."

"Believe me when I say, Jackie, I don't expect miracles from any man. One day, we will find the right men for us."

"It looks as though you may have found your Prince Charming—maybe."

"That's my hope, but it's not a sure thing. I'll see you later."

"Oh! Who's going to drive?" I was waiting for an answer, but I already knew what Nahiry would say. I also had my ulterior motive for wanting to be designated.

"You want to drive?" Nahiry asks.

"For a cozier ride, you and John should ride in the back while I drive. I want Craig in the front, where there won't be any ideas in the works."

"Okay, that's a good idea, and if I don't hit it off with John, I'll have a good excuse to leave with you and have a ride home."

"I don't know why you're thinking that way. You know you will hit it off. Anyway, I think I'm going to get dressed at your house. You have better jewelry than I do. I might even borrow some of your clothes."

"All right, Jackie. I'll see you later."

We part ways, and all I could think about was how annoying this dinner was going to be. The only positive thing about it would be the fact that Nahiry may have found her Prince Charming. And then it hit me. I'm still alone.

~

When I got home, I realized she was referencing my upcoming birthday of twenty-nine with the bowling lane. I guess because I didn't get it, she just left it alone. I checked my messages. "Hi, Jackie, this is your mother. You haven't called in two weeks. I want to hear from you. Have you found a nice man yet? Talk to you later." Nana is my aunt, my mother's sister. She took over raising us after our mother died. Nana had never married and had no children of her own, so she adopted us, but not in the legal sense.

She was so much like my mother, but she found no one she'd rather die for. *"Beep."*

'Jackie, this is Sharon. Have you spoken to Nahiry today? She was supposed to call me before you went bowling. If she comes over to your house, tell her to call me. Okay.' Thank goodness there were no more messages.

Sharon is Nahiry's sister. Although Nahiry's parents adopted Sharon when she was two, they had a wonderful relationship. Her parents died in a plane crash coming from Hawaii. She had no family that could take care of her, so they adopted her. They had all moved into my neighborhood when Nahiry was going on thirteen. Sharon was three years younger than the both of us.

Nahiry and I were always jealous of Sharon's good looks at a youthful age. She wanted to become a model, but she didn't have the height to pull it off. Among the three of us, Nahiry and I could wear one another's clothes. Sharon's were too little — except for her tops. Nahiry and I graduated together from high school and even took time off from school to go to Sharon's graduation. The best colors, royal blue and white, made Sharon's the best. Sharon won homecoming queen, and she wasn't a cheerleader, either. Sharon was strong-minded and knew she wanted a family and a husband to match in life.

Robert was a perfect nerd and fresh out of Jr. College when they were married and had Ashley Mariah. They were so happy over her arrival, Robert fainted in the delivery room, and Nahiry had to finish the job in helping Sharon deliver the baby. Her parents thought Sharon was all talk about marriage and kids, but she proved them wrong and got what she wanted out of life.

"Well, I better call Nana back. She'll be growing horns right about now."

'Hello, this is the Grimley residence. If you'll leave your name and number, we'll get back to you as soon as possible. Thank you and have a wonderful day. *Beep.*'

"Nana, this is Jackie. I'm sorry I haven't called sooner. I'll call you back later. Bye."

"No need to call Sharon back. She'll be talking to Nahiry right this minute."

After the exchange that happened today with Craig, I knew things were changing in my life. The once horrified feeling of telling people about my past and life was no longer a hinderance. I laughed after remembering the exchange with Dr. Simmons the day before.

Three o'clock arrived, and I head over to Nahiry's house. "Come on in. What clothes did you bring?" I was grinning as though I was working out a plan to deceive my non-date. I had this thing about naming my favorite clothes. Ms. Clara was my favorite black dress. Laughing wickedly.

"The one that shows your gorgeous figure. I thought you said you didn't like Craig?"

"I don't, but it doesn't mean I might not meet someone else there. Besides, I can at least make him drool. He's not the type to settle down. He wants a woman who he'll be able to jump into bed with and be at his disposal, and you know I don't go for that kind of thing." Nahiry noticed the deviousness, but she also knew my first experience with a man had not been a good one.

That conversation went like this long ago, "Jackie, the first time for women is always the worst, but as it progresses, it gets better and better."

"Well, believe me. The next time, it will be with my husband."

"So, you're a semi-virgin?" Nahiry laughs in that moment.

I looked back at her with that remark, "I guess you can say that." Talking about my first and only sexual experience didn't thrill me, and Nahiry knew my inexperience in that area. "So, let's get off the subject. I don't enjoy talking about my sex life or lack thereof."

"You just need to find the right person. A man who can open your eyes and heart. One that you can experience life with. Someone you don't have to pretend with. You can just be yourself."

"Well, if I find him, you will be the first to know." I tell her.

"I know, I better be."

Chapter 3

The Non-Date From Hell

THE DAY HAD BEEN BEAUTIFUL, but I was not into going on this date. I would've preferred to go on a date with someone I like or a good friend. Christopher made me laugh, but I found him unattractive in the sense. He didn't do it for me. He was also a clown, and I didn't want to be in love with a clown, although I regarded him as a good friend. Anyway, it was too late to back out of the agreement. One I wished I hadn't made to go out to dinner.

"Jackie, how long do you think it will take to get to John's house?"

"Not too long. He doesn't live far from you, per his address. We will eat at the Marina, so we won't have far to go. I hope we don't spoil this dinner for you two."

"Don't worry, I'll keep John occupied."

Pausing for a second, "You know you have a way with men. I have no clue how you do it. Even on blind dates, you seem to have an enjoyable time. You may not talk to them anymore, but you make the best of an unpleasant situation. I know for sure I can't be that pleasant."

Nahiry dancing in the mirror in her bedroom, "You know we don't have to rush, it's only three-thirty. We can leave at a quarter to six. I want to watch videos, anyway." Nahiry says before walking out of the room holding a dress that could kill if it was alive. Imagine if it was like Zorro.

"When did you get that dress? It's gorgeous. I thought you would wear that last black dress we went shopping for."

Nahiry exuding sexy, "I bought it last weekend. So, you weren't the only one buying something new." Nahiry turned back toward the room with a smug look on her face.

"I received a new book today. It's called, 'Forever Faith.' The first few pages seem to interest me, which is why I know it will be an exciting read. It was action packed, and I didn't have to wait an entire chapter before it got good."

"You mean the sex parts?"

"Yes, they make me laugh," I admitted.

"Well, if you were getting any, you wouldn't be laughing." Nahiry says. She pulled no punches with sex. She knew why I wasn't getting anywhere with men, and why I didn't like to think about it.

"Get out of here, Nahiry. A book can't make you horny, can it?"

"Yes, they can—if you knew what the feeling of ecstasy, passion, and intimacy was like. You've never had an orgasm in your life. You've only been with a man once, and that was nothing to be desired by any human being's standards. The only love you've ever known is with those kids at your office. I recognize the look on your face that you want a child. You almost cried when Sharon had Ashley. Missy, your attempts to deceive me are futile. I know you too well. You want a man who can love you and love children, too. That's something your father couldn't give you, and I hate to say it, but your own mother couldn't give you either."

"She tried to love me in her own way. As much as I hate to admit it, I see the same traits in Nana. She didn't have any choice but to take us in when my mother died. Some things are just passed down."

Concerned, "Jackie, knowing your mother only paid you any attention because your father wasn't in love with her, is not love. It was the acceptance that you were born. Your father cared more about his work than anything, and your mother cared more about your father than anything. It wasn't like she didn't have an option to leave. Jackie, you know all of this. I don't have to remind you." No, she never had to remind me of that fact. I thought about them every single day.

"Jackie, I can look at your face and know that you're in another world."

"Cynthia at work said the same thing." I never noticed my actions through other people's reactions.

"It's true. When I see you in that deep thought, I know you are thinking of your parents. You don't even talk to your brothers that often because they had more interaction with your father than you did, and you still resent them for it."

"I resent them, but it wasn't because of the attention they received, it was because as we got older, they didn't show me any love of their own. They treated me like my father did. After mom died and left most of the money to me, they disliked me even more. I was nothing to them—just like I was nothing to my father. I was just someone to cook and clean after them, like the way they thought about our mother. Whether they unconsciously imitated my father or it was ingrained in them, I vowed never to be like them. If I felt the way she did about us, I would never have children, but I don't feel that way.

I love kids, and I'd spoil them—but not to the point they're rotten. That's one reason I am very meticulous about not marrying someone who didn't want or could not love their child. I couldn't live with myself if I did. I think that's why I attached to you when we were growing up. You were the sister or even the brother I never had. Back then, I was the ugly duckling of the neighborhood. You didn't turn me away. You wanted to be my friend. Even as young as we were, I appreciated it then, and I still appreciate your friendship now."

"There's something different about you today, Jackie. I can't put my finger on it. You really stood up to Craig and his shenanigans. I've never seen you stand up for yourself that way. You were then as you are now: a sweet, original, innocent, and good friend. You helped me through some rough times too, you know. When we moved into the neighborhood, you came over to say hello. And when I got jealous of Sharon, you taught me her parents loved me, and they could love both Sharon *and* me, even though she wasn't my biological sister. You could have tainted me with how you were with your family, but you were the opposite. You know you were smart even back then, and you're still so smart. I never wanted to crush your innocence, and I never wanted to taint who you were as a person. There is one thing I want to say about your brothers. I know you blame them for not showing love to you, but as you have been around children for almost seven years now, you should know that children learn from what their parents do. If your father treated them as he treated you, well... you know where they learned their behavior. But you've grown up now, and so have they. They must be accountable for their relationships, and I am sorry to say, so are you. What I am trying to say is that you need to come to terms with your relationship with your brothers and see if they want to have a relationship with you. If every time you get on the phone you all argue, there is a miscommunication on both sides. I know you love your brothers, and maybe somewhere down deep in their hearts they may love you too, but don't cause your relationship with your brothers to deteriorate because of your father and mother's inability to love anyone but themselves. Jackie, you know I love you like you are my sister, but they are your flesh and blood. Make the first move to correct your relationship with them. This could have an adverse effect on how you perceive men. The bible says if you have an alt with your brother that you should go to him... or something like that."

The look on my face had to be one for the history books. "I have never heard you say anything closed to a bible scripture before. How do you know what it says?"

"I heard one of them televangelist preachers on the TV one morning after I let my ex spend the night. I didn't hear the whole sermon, but I got the gist of what he was saying."

I wanted to grin and smile to hide the truth, but I couldn't. "Well. You're pretty smart yourself, kid."

"Oh, you are trying to be the big sister, aren't you?" Nahiry laughs.

"Can I take a shower? I forgot when I was at home. I'm preoccupied with escaping your party.

~

As we were heading over to John's, the sun was setting like a lid closing on a cookie jar when we were little. As we arrived, I looked at the home. It once had a woman's touch. Of that, there was no doubt. The roses in front were now neglected, but the grass was green. Walking up to the door, I scoped out the neighborhood. This was the neighborhood I would love to one day raise children in. Kids running around playing with each other, trying to get the last bit of playing time before they had to go into their houses, because it was getting dark outside.

"Ring the bell, Nahiry." Before she could punch the button, the door swung open.

"Hi, John." Nahiry says. He looked at her as though he could eat her for dinner. He welcomed me in with a modest greeting.

"You both look great."

"Thank you very much. You look very handsome yourself," Nahiry replies.

As we were ready to sit on the couch, Craig walked out of the kitchen eating a full-fledged sandwich. Looking straight past him was a portrait of a woman. Her features were slim and becoming. She was beautiful, like something out of a fairytale. The picture intrigued me, so I headed toward the photograph and just stared. I bypassed Craig without saying nothing, and he followed behind me.

"Excuse me, excuse me. Can I help you?"

I hesitated before answering his rudeness. Maybe I was the rude one. It was John's house. "Who is this?"

"It's my mother."

Moving closer to the portrait, "She's exquisite."

"Yes, she was." By his comment, I knew this incredibly beautiful woman was no longer walking this earth.

"She's been gone for many years," he says.

"Did she pass away young?"

He leaned up against the table near the picture. "If you call thirty-seven young, then yes," he answers with a caring voice.

"Yes, I consider that young. I'm sorry for your loss. You miss her, don't you?" I could tell my question frustrated him. Only my assumption was that he never talked about his mother much to other than with his brother. Craig turned to look at himself one more time in a mirror that was in the kitchen. *What a weird place to have a mirror*, I thought.

"Can we go eat now? I only agreed to go because of my brother."

"Well, now I don't have to feel guilty." Expressing my disdain for his presence. I walked out of the room without even looking back at him.

Nahiry tells me later that John expressed, "It seems Craig has met his match. Someone who has the brains and the looks." John motions to Nahiry as we were leaving.

"This will be an interesting night, won't it?"

"Yes, John, I think so."

They were both men with some manners and opened the car doors for us both. The drive to the restaurant was quiet in the front and all talk and laughter in the back. The hostess seated us at a table near an ocean view. John pulled out Nahiry's chair, and before Craig could pull out mine, I sat down and just left him standing there, wanting to make sure he knew this was not a date, and I was making sure the whole restaurant knew *the same*. The night went on with pleasant conversation. Nahiry and John were getting along great when I noticed someone coming toward the table, but I didn't look up to see who. He spoke in a deep, caring voice as he always did, "Hello, Jacqueline." My eyes locked on his. I grinned when I saw who it was. "Hello, Dr. Simmons." He came back at me, clearly fed up with my Dr. Simmons bit. "You know what, Jackie? I'm going to dock your pay for continuing to call me Dr. Simmons." I had to laugh, knowing he wouldn't do that to me. "All right. I'll call you Dr. John."

"Well, at least it's a start." He glanced at the table, looking at the two couples. "How is the evening going? Well, I hope?" he asks.

I waited a few seconds to answer. "It's okay. Oh, excuse my manners. Dr. Simmons, I mean Dr. John, this is Craig and his brother John, and you know Nahiry."

"Yes, I do. Nice to see you again, Nahiry." Dr. John stuck out his hand to both John and Craig.

"It was nice meeting you. A namesake as well. I must return to my table."

"Who is it tonight, if I may ask?" He turned his attention to me. "Why are you jealous?" I let out a giggle and tried to conceal my embarrassment. "Come on, Dr. Simmons, give me a break." He turned toward Nahiry. "Well, just for calling me Dr. Simmons, see you later, Nahiry. Jacqueline, I'll see you early Monday morning, and gentlemen, it was a pleasure."

"You won't tell me, will you?" As he walked away, out of hearing range, "He'll tell me Monday, anyway."

"So, he's your boss?" Craig asks with a smirk.

"Yes, he is. Why?" He bypassed her question. "So, what kind of doctor is he?" I know he was just trying to make conversation, because John and Nahiry were so into each other. They didn't even finish their meals. "He's an OB-GYN. He also runs his own pediatric clinic." Craig sat back in his seat and stared at me with his probing eyes.

"He's pretty young, isn't he? To be a full-fledged doctor already?"

"Not really. He just looks younger than he is."

"How old is he?"

"He's thirty-eight. Why all the questions about Dr. Simmons?" He put his elbows on the table.

"Because of the way you looked at him. It seems as if there was more than an employer-employee relationship." I was never one to show my emotions, but these days, I was having no problem with expressing them. "Well, there isn't and never has been. I have nothing more than admiration and respect for Dr. Simmons. Now, can we get off the subject and finish eating?" He would not let up. I could see it coming. He was trying my patience. "No problem." Nahiry, looking into my eyes, knew all too well, the questions Craig had asked aggravated me, but she kept it to herself for the moment. Probing more, Nahiry had since noticed I had calmed down and was in a relaxed mood. She wasn't suspecting anything else to come out of Craig's mouth.

"Jackie, what do you do for ole doc Simmons?"

I decided not to look up at him as I ate my dessert. "I am a Pediatric RN, and I work in his clinic."

"I know assistants do not get paid that much, so how are you able to drive a Jaguar?"

My fork slammed down on the table, and the people next to us turned slightly. "Oh, no!" Nahiry says. Before she could calm me down, my ears and cheeks turned red. "I have had it with you. You are a self-centered, egotistical, chauvinistic pig. Are you implying something? Because if you are, let me tell you something worthwhile hearing. I work for a living. I do not need a man to give me money, and I sure as hell don't need you trying to pry into my personal life. Anyway, it is none of your business why I drive a Jag or how I get the money to pay for it, or how I got the money to pay for your dinner. Excuse me, I'm going to the lady's room. You want to know what I'm going to do in there too?" Nahiry followed me, and Craig sat there in unbelief. All John could do was hold his head in his hands. "Jackie, what is going on? I have never seen you act like this before."

I looked Nahiry in the eyes, and the waterworks rolled. "Nahiry, I don't know what's wrong with me. I'm falling apart. I was so optimistic this morning and now I'm crying, because I feel empty, and being here with a man I despise with every fiber of my being proves that point."

I know Nahiry wanted to be the voice of reason, but she could not take this burden from me.

"Jackie, didn't we have this same discussion before we left the house? Listen to me, there are no perfect men in this world, and neither are there any perfect women. But when a man and a woman click, it's wonderful. You just haven't found him yet. And when you do, you will love him with all your heart and soul. Plus, I know you won't click with a man like Craig. As far as this whole situation is concerned, though, I believe you overreacted a bit. You haven't given him a chance to hang himself, you've judged him on first impressions alone. Yes, he is sarcastic and arrogant, but show him something different. If you can't, I understand, but to attract different, you must be different. Be yourself, but you can't allow men like him to make you act out of character. He had bad breath anyway!" I let out a cry-giggle, and Nahiry continues, "This is what I want you to do. Go out there with your head up high and tell the world you're available."

As I wiped my tears away, my voice was shaky but slowly becoming normal. "Okay! So, go out there and be yourself and pay no attention to the jerk." I pulled my dress straight and re-applied my face paint. I turned toward Nahiry. "Nahiry, I just want to say I'm so sorry for messing up your evening." We hugged.

"Oh, don't worry about it. John's coming over after you drop them off."

"Well, I'll say it again. I think you've found your Prince Charming for the hundredth time."

"I don't know, but this sure feels different."

"Nahiry, just promise me you won't sleep with him tonight. Wait, a while to see if he wants you for you and not just your body. I don't want to see you get hurt again." Nahiry turned toward the mirror. "Don't worry. I'm not jumping in the sack with anybody. Not with all these STDs going around. Let's go, Jackie, and keep your chin up."

When we reached the table, everyone was quiet. "Is everything all right, madam?" the server asked.

I cleared my throat with some embarrassment. "Yes, it was just a little misunderstanding. We would like the check, please."

"Yes, right away, madam."

~

On the way home, no one spoke a word. As I pulled up to John's house, "Before you both get out, I just want to apologize for my outburst. I'm embarrassed for my reaction and I overreacted." Craig got out of the car and says nothing. John acknowledged my apology and told me not to worry about it. As I was sitting there waiting for Nahiry to get back into the car, a sigh of relief came over me that the night was over. Understanding tonight was the worst night ever, I arrived home, took off my clothes and left them right there on the floor. I ran the bath water while sitting in the tub and sank my head under to washing the entire night away. After figuring out my schedule for the next day, which included exercise, maybe church, since Cynthia had been asking me to go, I slid into bed to sleep.

~

The next morning, '*I don't feel like doing exercises, I don't feel like going to church, and I'll call Nana later. I've got to get to the dry cleaners, though. I'm going to lounge around for a change, sit on the patio, and read my new book,*' were the thoughts in my head.

In the last chapter, when I looked at my watch, "Three o'clock. Oh, no!" The dry cleaner's is closed. Well, at least I have a clean coat here. This book was wonderful.

Chapter 4

The Elaborate Invite

ANOTHER YEAR HAD PAST and with only two weeks till my birthday. I wanted nothing special, since I was only getting older, and with no man in my life, I wasn't up for having a big bash, announcing to the world I was turning thirty and had no date for my party. I didn't want further reminders by inviting a bunch of couples to come over, either. Nahiry and John continued seeing each other, and Jerry was out of the picture completely. Craig got the girl of his dreams—a twit—but at least he wasn't alone.

Arriving at work, Cynthia says, "Jackie, you received a call from Nahiry. She said to call her back. It's important."

"Okay, Cynthia." Looking through my other messages, none were important. Before I could reach my office, Cynthia stopped me with my hand on the knob.

"Dr. Simmons also wants to see you."

"Okay, thank you." Instead of going into my office, I went straight to Dr. Simmons. I knocked on his door and wondered what was wrong. He never asked Cynthia to tell me to come to his office before. I would either just go or he would come to mine. Pushing the door open, I saw him hanging up the phone.

"Hello, Jacqueline, come in."

Sitting, I gave my morning greeting, "Good Morning."

He leaned back in his chair with a simple grin. "Dr. John. You know that's kind of cute. How are you doing this morning?"

I relaxed a little, but my curiosity still didn't wane. "I'm doing fine."

He stood up from his desk. "I guess you're wondering why I called you in here."

"Yes, curious. You never ask me to come to your office. I just come in or you come to my office."

He sat back down. "I'm aware, but the reason I've asked you to come to my office is because..."

I didn't even let him finish what he wanted to say. "Oh, no! You're not firing me, are you? I love this job."

He grinned. "No, Jackie, I'm not firing you." I'm sure he sensed the urgency in my voice, but before he could reassure or denounce my fears, I started again.

"Did I do something wrong?"

Now he was laughing. "No, you did nothing wrong. Would you be quiet for a minute, so I can finish what I wanted to ask?" I sat silent and still. "I called you in here to ask you if you would like to go out on a date with me?"

Now I sat quietly with my poker face. "I'm flattered, but I can't."

His grin went to curiosity. "Why not? The reason I asked was that I'm not seeing anyone right now."

"Actually, you haven't been dating for about a month now."

"Oh! You're keeping tabs of my dating life, are you?"

I wanted to crawl under the desk, but I had to be a grownup. "No! It's just that you haven't brought one to the office for me to comment on—in that period."

***

(Here is where the tide turns, and to tell part of the story, this is Dr. John. I need to take charge because she wasn't informed, so we'll need to communicate frequently from now on.)

A simple smile. I stared at her for a second and then brought myself back to what I wanted to say. "Anyway, there is a party for one of my colleagues on the twenty-first of this month, and I don't feel like taking an ex-girlfriend. I don't want the hassle of someone hanging all over me."

"Well, thank you for thinking about me, but my birthday is that day, and I don't know if I'm going to have any plans. I may invite you to my party, as well."

I didn't know why she tells that fib. She didn't know I knew she didn't want to have a party. "Well, you think about it, and if you change your mind, can you let me know a few days before? Oh, and if can go, I'll throw in a birthday dinner."

She stood and walked to the door. "Thank you. I'll think about it and let you know if I have no other plans."

I walked out of the office, stunned. I looked up toward the sky, but it was the clinic ceiling. *'Am I that pitiful? My boss is feeling sorry for me.'* I thought. That's what I took from the entire conversation. Was it my purpose in life for people to feel sorry for me?

"Jackie, what's wrong?" Cynthia asks, concerned.

"He asked me out on a platonic date on my birthday."

"That's great." Cynthia was excited for me.

"No, it's not great."

"Why would you say that?"

"Knowing my friend Nahiry, she will throw me a party or a get together, like she does every year. She will be disappointed if she can't."

"Maybe you should call her and ask if she would mind not throwing you a party this year or just postpone it?"

I pondered that thought for a minute. "Yes, I could, but I know Nahiry. She lives for parties. What am I going to do?"

By my response, Cynthia realized I was thinking about saying yes, but I changed my mind. "Well, going out on a platonic date with someone you know might be a good thing. It will get you out there and help you get to know what's out there with no hassle."

"Well, I don't know…"

***

As Jaqueline walked into her office, Cynthia headed to mine. The knock she gave was loud enough for me to hear only. "Dr. Simmons." She closed the door behind her.

"She's considering not going out with you."

"I thought so, but I couldn't come up with anything right then. You better get Nahiry on the phone," I requested.

"Okay, will do." With Nahiry on the phone, she buzzed my office. "Nahiry's on line one." She didn't want to take any chances of Jackie overhearing her.

"Hello, Nahiry."

"Hello, John. Did you get her to go out with you?"

I hesitated before answering. "No, not yet. We may have to go to Plan B. She's thinking about you giving her a birthday party again."

Nahiry sighs, "Okay! I'll convince her. I'll call you at home after I talk to her."

~

Nahiry called me right away. "Jacqueline, line one. It's Nahiry." Cynthia says.

"Hi, Nahiry, what's going on?"

Excitement from Nahiry wasn't shocking. It was often Nahiry called me with news. She couldn't wait to tell me, "You'll never believe it." Nahiry hesitated before going on and then giggled. "John has asked me to marry him, and we're getting married on the twentieth of this month, and on the same day we're flying to the Bahamas."

It stunned me, to say the least. I went silent. After about 20 seconds, I decided I had better say something. "You're getting married, that's great. Oh, no, that's in two weeks, Nahiry. How are we going to plan a wedding in two weeks? I'm coming over to your house after I get off."

For a moment, I reflected on the entire situation. I wasn't being a good friend. I was thinking about myself and my birthday and Nahiry not being there for me this time. What I was thinking was selfish. Something my parents would say or do. I finally came out of my selfishness. "Oh my God, you are getting married. I am so excited for you!" We both screamed with excitement, and the entire office could hear. But now I didn't have an excuse not to go with Dr. John on my birthday.

"I'm sorry, Jackie. I know I was supposed to give you a party. But this time you understand, don't you?"

"Of course, I do. What kind of question is that?"

"Oh! Jackie, I'm so happy I could burst. Jackie, I want you to be my Maid-of-Honor."

"I would love to. You know you're my best friend — my sister. I wouldn't be anyplace else, then by your side."

"Thank you, Jackie. You're going to make me cry."

"Oh, stop it. Cry on your wedding day, not now. I'll see to you later, okay! I have to finish some paperwork."

Yes, I admit, I was disappointed that I wouldn't have a party, but more importantly, someone else was getting married before me—again, reflecting my selfish thoughts. I had to be ecstatic for Nahiry and get over my hang-ups. She had finally found true love with an honest man—her Prince Charming.

***

It was almost time to head home. So, she stopped by my office.

"Dr. John."

"Come in, Jacqueline. Can I help you with something?"

"Well, I guess I'm going to help you out. I want to take you up on your offer. Nahiry is getting married that Friday, and she won't be able to give me a party. So, I'm all yours. I mean, I can go to the party with you."

"I'm glad you can go—even though it's at the expense of not having a party of your own." She tried not to show her disappointment, but I could see. She put on a noble face. But I had to wonder why she was not as excited for Nahiry as I thought she should be. "Oh, it's nothing. If I know my friend, she'll throw a grand party at her reception."

He stood with his masculine body from his chair and there were certain things about him I hadn't noticed before. But he broke my thought. "Well, the party won't start until eight o'clock. So, I'll pick you up at six, and we can have your birthday dinner like I promised." I stood too and headed to the door. "That sounds nice. I will enjoy myself in your company."

"Sure, and we can get to know each other a little better outside of work circumstances. Oh, the party is formal, by the way. So, wear your best dress."

She smiled. "Okay, see you tomorrow."

***

An hour later, "Cynthia, is Jacqueline gone?"

"Yes, sir."

"Oh, would you stop calling me sir? My name is John."

"Okay, Dr. Simmons."

"Get Nahiry on the line. She's going to be my date for the party. I also may need your help, and if you need to leave early, then that is fine with me. Let's work on our scheduling tomorrow."

~

Jackie spent the next week and a half making plans with Nahiry. It would be a small chapel wedding with only a few family members. They picked clothes out of the closet to wear for the wedding, so no shopping for dresses. They would later have a big reception once they got back from their honeymoon. There would be no frills for the day of the wedding, but for the party, they would do it big.

Chapter 5

Surprises

TWO DAYS BEFORE THE WEDDING, I head to Nahiry's house to go over any last-minute details we should go over. When I reached the front door, I could hear sobbing. "Nahiry, come open the door." Though muffled, I understood her voice. "I'm coming." She opens the door, and puddles of tears were on her cheeks. "Nahiry, what's going on?" As she closed the solid wooden door, Nahiry cries again, "John called the wedding off."

"What! Why did he do that? We've prepared for your wedding!" Her body groveled to the chair near the black velvet couch. "Because he said he wasn't ready to get married yet and tied down with one woman." I slid closer to give her some comfort.

"That doesn't sound like John. In fact, it sounds more like my boss, or Craig."

"I know, but when I went to his house to pick up a dress I had left, a girl opened the door in his pajama top." My blood was boiling. "Ooh! Men are such dogs. Why do we need them? I'm sorry, Nahiry, stop crying. You're going to get a headache you can't get rid of." Nahiry stood from the chair and walked to the front window. "I've made all these plans, and now I can't use any of them. I jumped at him too much, didn't I?"

"Nahiry, none of this is your fault. You loved him. He just didn't want to love you back."

I believed every word. Nahiry sobbed even the more for another thirty minutes. I didn't know a person could cry that much. The reality of all this sank in. If John were like this, what was waiting for me?

"Come on, Nahiry, lay down and get some rest. Tomorrow or next week, you'll be refreshed to find a real man for you. Like you always do, you will overcome this setback.

"Jackie, this hurts worse than Kenny. I only loved Kenny for the sex. It was different with John. I loved him with all my heart. Jackie, I don't want you to have to stop what you're doing. Go do your thing and I'll be fine. I will make it through this. I just want to be alone right now. Please, I'll call you later, okay?"

"I don't mind. I'd do anything for you, you know that. I'll call you tomorrow after work. Get some sleep."

Nahiry closed her eyes. "I will."

***

Hey, Nahiry, here. I wanted to put my two scents into what went down that day. I should have been an actress. My Oscar was waiting in the wings. Anyway, I jumped off the couch as soon as I heard the front door slam, watching as she drove away. My John pulls up as Jackie turned the corner. I shrieked, as I hoped she didn't see him. I walk out to the end of the porch to meet him. Hurrying him to move it into the house.

"I saw Jackie leave. Did she buy it?"

"Like a loaf of bread, my sweet." We both walk in the house in lip-lock.

"We are pulling off the ultimate surprise party."

"You know, after this party. We will make plans of our own." He hugs me.

"Well, you had better get on the horn to Dr. Simmons."

"On it right now."

"You know they would make a good couple." I turned to John, "Who are you talking about?" His forehead seemed to cringe. "Jackie and Dr. Simmons."

"I can't see it."

"Why can't you see it Nahiry? It's so obvious she likes him."

"I don't see it because Jackie is very adamant about not mixing business with pleasure."

"Well then, why did she accept a dinner and party invitation?"

Puzzled... "I guess she didn't want to be alone. Besides, Dr. Simmons is harmless. Why do you think I called him and asked him to do this? She will be his date for the evening, and it's platonic."

"I have a feeling. Things just might change for her."

"Oh! Quit trying to be a matchmaker. I'll call Dr. Simmons and tell him everything is a go."

***

The phone rang in my library. "Hey, Dr. John, this is Nahiry. I finished putting the last touches on our plan. We don't have to worry about a wedding."

I smile out of the oval window next to my desk, as a Jaybird was sitting on the fence. "Oh! By the way, I will have Cynthia drop my house keys off to you tomorrow night. I'll rent a hotel room, so I won't be in your way."

"Sincerely, John. That's very generous of you, but I don't want to inconvenience you."

"You're not, Nahiry. It was my suggestion to use my house, wasn't it? So, don't worry about me."

"Okay. To cover my tracks, I will call Jackie and tell her I'm going away for a few days, so she won't wonder where I am."

"Nahiry, I wanted to ask what's the color scheme for the party?"

"The colors are purple, white, and black. Purple is Jackie's' favorite color. She loves Amethyst."

"Oh, yes, she was born on the cusp in February. Thanks for reminding me."

"No problem at all. Just get her to the party at eight-thirty!"

"Count on it, and I will talk to you tomorrow."

~

Friday afternoon, a little before the end of the workday, I checked in with Dr. John to see if the plans were still in order. I hesitated to knock, hearing him talking on the phone, but I poked my head in the door. "Oh, it's you! Just the person I wanted to see. We need to go over our plans for tomorrow," he says, covering the mouthpiece with his hand.

I sat in the chair, waiting for him to finish his conversation on the phone. "Sorry for the delay. The party tomorrow, I found out it's very formal. I wanted to know if you had a gown to wear?"

I went into an instant panic. "No, I don't. I thought you said just wear a dress. I guess I can pick one up before the store closes."

"Oh, no! Don't do that. Would you give me the honor of picking something out for you? Just say it's a birthday gift."

"I can't let you do that."

"Jacqueline. You're doing me a favor by going out with me tomorrow. I figured I would do this for your birthday, anyway. Please let me do this for you?"

How could I say no after that plea? "How can I refuse such a gracious offer like that?" This confirmed my suspicion of being pitied. He stood and smiled. "Thank you very much. I know what kind of taste you like. I'll send it over tomorrow morning. Oh, I need your size!" Now I stood to my feet and looked straight into his eyes. "It's an eight." Before I could reach the door, he adds, "And if you need any tailoring, there will be a Seamstress coming. And thank you again for accepting my gift. I hope you like what I pick out."

"I'm sure I will."

"Thank you, again, Jacqueline."

"You don't have to thank me anymore, Dr. John, it's my pleasure."

"I'm sorry for acting like a teenager, but I am honored you're allowing me to do this for you."

"Believe me, I wouldn't let you do this if it wasn't my birthday."

~

I walked out of his office and over to Cynthia's desk. "Cynthia, he's buying me a gown for my birthday."

"That's great, Jackie! Have you seen it?"

"No, he's going to send it to my house in the morning, with a seamstress to go with it."

"Wow. This is so exciting, Jackie. I hope you have a wonderful time tomorrow for your birthday."

"Thank you."

"Oh! I didn't tell you the news. I'm engaged."

"That's wonderful, congratulations." This time, I was genuinely excited for Cynthia. I had learned my lesson with Nahiry. Just be there for your friends.

"Now there are two couples you know that are getting married."

"Nahiry is not getting married anymore."

"What happened?"

"Her fiancé called off the wedding. Nahiry found him with another woman. You know, I never figured John to be that type of man. You just never know what they'll do next. Being careful is not enough these days. I'm leaving now. I have to wake up early in the morning."

"Jackie, are you all right?"

"I'm fine. I just need some good sleep."

~

I got home and flopped on my bed and slept for six hours straight. Waking, it was already midnight. "Ha! It's your birthday, kid. You're thirty and still no man." What depressing knowledge. It wasn't all bad. I was getting a new gown for my birthday. At least I won't be totally alone. I had time to think about all that had transpired for the past two weeks. Reflecting on my life and thinking about some conversations I had with Nahiry. I truly hadn't been a good friend. Even though they wouldn't be getting married. I was jealous that Nahiry had found the man of her dreams and wasn't genuinely happy for her, because then I would truly be alone. I had everything, but it wasn't enough to just be. I had some serious soul searching to do. This loneliness was consuming me and it wasn't making me happy about how I had been acting.

I walk into the living room to check my messages. *'Beep.'*

"Jackie, hi, it's Nahiry. Sorry, but I won't be here for your birthday. I'm going away for a couple of days to get my mind straight and my life back in order. Please understand and don't worry about me. Once I get to my destination, I will let you know I've arrived safely. Have a wonderful birthday, and I promise to make it up to you when I get back, and next year. See you later."

'Beep. You have no more messages.'

"What shall I do now? My friend is hurting, and I can't do anything for her. She didn't even tell me where she was going. I can't go back to sleep—I'll take a relaxing bath."

Three-thirty in the morning came. I slept until seven o'clock, when the doorbell woke me. Running to the door, I open it abruptly.

"Hello, are you Jacqueline?"

"Yes, you must be from the dress shop."

"Yes, my name is Monica, and I'm here to help you with any tailoring you may need. I have the dress Dr. Simmons picked for you."

"Yes, can I see it? I'm dying to look at it."

"I believe it's your favorite color, Dr. Simmons remarked." Monica pulls out the gown from the garment bag.

"Oh, my goodness, this is gorgeous!"

"It's made of Amethyst Velvet, and I've brought the shoes to match."

I lifted the gown to my body as I stood in front of her mirror. "This is too much. I can't believe it."

The doorbell rang again, and I gave the gown to Monica and walked to the door. "Hello, can I help you?" A man stood smiling before me, looking devilishly handsome and honest. He spoke in an English accent. "Yes. Is this the Mason residence?" A little reluctant—I answer, "Yes, this is the Mason residence. Can I help you?"

"My name is Edward. I'm a representative of Aryl Jewelers. Dr. Simmons requested I bring these to you. He also requested I explain to you these are on loan, but they would go well with your gown. He also said you wouldn't accept them if I didn't explain this to you. May I come in?"

"Absolutely, you may." Slowly reaching my hands to sit on the couch in front of the coffee table, Edward opened the box. My eyes opened as wide as any eyes could to the Amethyst sparkle.

"There is also a bracelet to match the necklace underneath the padding." I was in a daze and couldn't shake it off for a minute.

High noon came, and sweat was pouring. My hands were shaking in anticipation, and my stomach was in my throat. "Why did Nahiry have to leave?" *She should be here to help me,* I thought. I have a hair and nail appointment at one o'clock. I'm nervous and can't believe it. It's only my boss. But why would he go through all this trouble just for some party? He must keep his image up, I guess. I don't understand.

He could have gotten any of his floozies to go with him. I guess, like he said, he didn't want the hassle. But he asked you, Jacqueline. Why?

Five o'clock came and so did a phone call.

"Hello, John."

"Oh! My goodness, she finally called me John! I presume you have received everything to your satisfaction?"

"Oh, yes, yes, I did."

"So, how do you like them?"

"John, everything is gorgeous. You did a wonderful job of picking out everything. And the jewels, I'm just in awe! I've never seen such a brilliant amethyst before." Pausing, I realize I was acting like a schoolgirl.

"I figured you would like them. How did the dress fit?"

"It fit, perfectly. There were no changes needed. How did you know Amethyst was my favorite color?"

"Jackie, you wear it all the time. Your class ring even has that stone in it. How could I not know?"

"Was I that predictable?"

"Only when you wear purple almost every day. Oh! You thought I hadn't noticed. Well, I notice. I notice everything about you." There was an awkward silence. "Well, I had better let you go. I'll pick you up at six o'clock."

"Okay. I'll be ready."

I was feeling happy and caught myself. I went to my closet in the full-length mirror. The Amethyst sparkled in the light, glimmering from the sun, setting off the mirror. I would never have gone this extravagant—even though I could afford to buy it and more. I finally felt beautiful. I was now having no regret in accepting the date. I knew I would have a decent time. Dr. Simmons was always joking around and playing pranks on the staff, so I knew he was fun. I put all of my fears behind me, as I remembered what Cynthia tells me, *'Jackie, open your eyes and your heart. Try anything once and don't give up on your dreams.'*

One thing was for sure. I hadn't given up on my dreams, and one day I would find the right man for me.

Chapter 6

Where Do We Go From Here?

AN ALL-WHITE LIMO ARRIVED in front of the house. The streetlights and the setting sun shone on a man who would not ordinarily excite me to the point of having butterflies in my stomach. Tonight was an exception. It didn't take long for the neighbors to come out of their homes to see what was going on, even Ms. Abner. I didn't want to seem anxious. I step away from my front window and wait until he rang the doorbell to let him in. Slowly opening the door, his eyes were wide in amazement. "You look beautiful." I bowed and curtseyed like a princess would. "Why thank you, kind sir. You look very handsome and debonair yourself."

***

As I shook the gaze, my hand rose to meet her lovely face. "This is for you. A single white rose for the birthday lady."

She inhaled the fragrance of the flower. "Thank you, John. Will you come in, so I can get my bag?" she says.

She walked out of my sight. "This is a lovely house." I looked around at the pictures on the wall and on the mantle when she came back in. "This is your mother and father in the picture?"

"Yes, I kept most of the photographs of my parents after they died and some antique furniture." She looked at me with a little shame in her eyes. I could see the pain and wanted to say something — but didn't. "I guess we better go."

As she walked to the door, I caught up to her and opened the door. "The night is young, and you will have fun — if it's the last thing I do."

"I'm sure we will."

~

A host seated us immediately in the restaurant. "Would you like to hear our specials today?" The server asked. Smiling from ear to ear.

"No, thank you. I know what we want."

"Okay, what would you like?" he asks.

John glanced over at Jacqueline. "We would like two double bacon cheeseburgers, one large order of onion rings, and two strawberry fountain sodas. That will be all, thank you."

"Thank you for your order, and I'll bring your drinks right over."

I stared at him in unbelief. A Jewish OB-GYN ordered bacon for his burger, but that's not what I focused on. "I can't believe you brought me to a burger joint. Everyone is staring at us."

"Don't pay them any attention. We're here to have dinner and enjoy ourselves. I figured you'd been to every Marina restaurant, anyway. So, here we are at the place that has the best burgers in town."

"Let me get this straight. You bought me a gown, borrowed jewels, and rented a limo to bring me to eat hamburgers. You're joking, right?" I put my hands over my face to cover the embarrassment.

"This is no joke, Jacqueline. I know for a fact you go bowling for fun, and your favorite food is burgers. There's nothing wrong with that, but you should relax and live a little. You like bacon on your hamburgers, don't you?"

I hesitated to answer, "Yes." Smiling largely behind my embarrassment.

"And you like the gown and parties, don't you?"

"Yes, but."

"No buts. You will enjoy this evening, even if it kills me."

There was nothing else to lose from here. "You're strange, John, but I like it." I exhale. "Okay! I will relax and have an enjoyable time. Even if it kills me. Forgive me for being a temporary bourgeoisie ingrate. I get stuck in my routines, and I don't live for the moment. That stops right here and now."

Our second stop was at the beach to watch the sun take its bow. We didn't get out of the limo, but stood up through the sunroof. The night sky pierced with bright stars and a clear, moon-lit night, and we talked about any and everything. Sitting in the limo at the beach, we really got to know each other.

***

Arriving at eight-fifteen, I told the limo driver to park. "Shouldn't we get out, so he can park?" she asks.

"No, I don't want to walk in too early. They will announce us at this party, so I want to be fashionably late, with the most beautiful woman right beside me. And that is definitely no joke." She smiles uncontrollably at me with a gleam of brightness I'd never seen before. I was pleased to see her smile and to know it was genuine. "You have a wonderful smile. I hope to see it more often."

"This night so far has proven to be something to smile about." She says.

It stayed quiet for the time being in the limo. I knew I had more than admiration for John, but I dared not say anything. "It is eight twenty-eight. Shall we go now?" I ask.

"Yes," he replies softly.

As we walked in, they drew the curtain upon our announcement. I was nervous, but it quickly subsided when he glanced across and smiled at me. "I want you to know I have never been to a party like this." The man then announced after receiving the invitation, "Please welcome Miss. Jacqueline Mason and Dr. John Simmons." The curtain drew back. "Surprise! Happy Birthday!"

It seemed like I held my breath for a year as the tears fell. I grabbed his hand with almost love. "You are good. Thank you." I kissed him on the lips, and it startled both of us, but I'm the one who pulled away, smiling. He walks me down the stairs to greet everyone. I was nervously crying and giggling at the same time. Nahiry met us at the bottom of the stairs. "I could kill you for lying. John, she had me calling you a dog, a pig, and everything other than a cuss word." Nahiry was dabbing the tears from my face. "Thank you so much for everything. This is one party I'll never forget. And how did you get this handsome doctor to go along with this surprise?"

Nahiry laughed. "Oh, Jackie, it was so easy. I called him up, and he gave me the keys to his house."

"This is your house?"

"Yes. I knew you had never seen it, so it was the perfect place to have a surprise party."

***

I gestured around Jacqueline of my approval to what Nahiry had done to my house. "So, how do you like your decorations?"

"So, this's how you found out my favorite colors."

"I must confess. I wasn't 100 percent sure. I had to confirm it with Nahiry. And she did a fantastic job with this old house."

"Why thank you, but it was nothing at all. I had a little help from John, Sharon, and Craig." Nahiry says.

"Craig! Is he here?" Jackie asks.

"He couldn't make it — hot date."

"Well, thank him when you get home, John, and thank you all again. This is so great. This is a most special birthday."

Nahiry's John grabbed her arm and gestured to Jackie, "I will have to take my girl and leave you to your party now." As they turned and left, I turn to Jacqueline. "Would you care to dance?" She watched me intently.

"Yes, I would love too."

"Follow me."

On the dance floor, I embraced her, and held her with compassion and love that I'd never felt with any other woman, and she didn't resist. "Thank you for giving up your home." She says. I kept my face at the side of hers. "It was my pleasure." No more words came. We held each other as though we had been married for fifty-years.

~

On the other side of the room, John was dancing with Nahiry and looking over at Dr. John and Jacqueline.

"Nahiry?"

"What is it, John?"

"I told you they made a good couple," he says with a smile.

"I guess you were right all along." Still holding on to John, she glances our way. "Yes, maybe so, but the night is still young."

~

Saying goodnight to the last guest, we walk back into the house. "So, does this mean our date has ended also?" I ask.

"Not unless you want it to be over?" she says.

"I don't think I would have asked if I wanted it to end."

"Point well taken, and so, what would you like to do now?"

I look outside into the backyard. "Shall we take a stroll in the garden?"

"Yes, I would like that."

We walk more, smelling the fragrance of the flowers. I could feel his hand linger behind me as he slowed down to speak. "Jacqueline, can I ask you a question and get a straight answer?"

"Yes, John."

He looked up to the stars, and I briefly did too. "How is it you don't have a man in your life?"

Again hesitant, "To tell you the truth, I couldn't say. It's not that I don't want a man in my life. Maybe I expect too much. I don't express it, but I'm looking for the man my father wasn't. Cynthia once told me I shouldn't be looking, but that God would send the man I would spend the rest of my life with, that *he* would find me. At first, I didn't take it to heart what she said, but I want to believe there is someone out there for me. A part of me doesn't believe that *he* will ever find me, though."

"So, why did you really agree to go out with me tonight?"

"I knew this date was on the up and up. You said you needed a date for your colleague's party. So, I said yes. Plus, in all honesty, who wants to be alone on their birthday?"

***

My body withdrew from hers. "Jacqueline." Her eyes rose to mine. "You do not know, do you?"

"Idea about what? What are you talking about?" I pull her close and we kiss again. I never wanted to stop, but she suddenly pulls away. "I must go."

"Why do you have to leave? Don't you know how I feel about you after all this time?"

I could see hurt pouring to the forefront of her mind. "I'm sorry. Can the limo take me home?" There was disappointment in his eyes and in the sagging of his body. It hurt me to see him that way. I reached out to him in my mind, but my body didn't respond the same. "Yes, of course. I'll tell him to take you home." He grabbed my arm softly to turn me toward him. "Can't you trust me enough to tell me what's wrong?" He wanted an explanation if I would give one. "I will explain, but not now. I have to go." His hand slid down my arm, and I walked away in tears.

~

On the way home, I cried in silence. The limo pulls in front of my home, and I thanked him.

"Miss. Mason, have a good rest of your night and happy birthday."

"Goodnight, Robert, and thank you for the evening."

"You're welcome, Miss. Mason."

I could hardly drag myself in the front door, but I managed. I was coherent enough to put the gown back into the garment bag and flop onto the bed — face down. My pain rolled from the corner of my eye, across my nose and down my other cheek. "Why couldn't I tell him how I felt?" This was the first time I ever talked to God and prayed. My mind ran with so many questions. I didn't know if God was listening or I was being stupid for talking to someone I didn't know existed. Was it I didn't know how I felt, or was I too afraid to feel? All this time, I've wanted someone to love. Someone who would love me in the same way. John was there. A man had opened his heart to me, and I couldn't handle it. I was afraid that as much as I wanted this, I couldn't give him what he needed. I was afraid I would be my parents.

Chapter 7

Making the Right Decision

NOT WAKING UNTIL that next afternoon. "Why did I sleep this long? I still feel horrible." I rose, and my head pounded like a sledgehammer was whacking it all night. Last night, I drank too much. I had my first hangover, and so I gently fall back onto the pillow. The piercing peach aroma—from the potpourri I placed on my night table the day before was not helping my situation. I almost drifted back to sleep when the doorbell rang. Startled, I jerked upright as the increasingly loud doorbell rang again. I took a slight jog to the front door. I opened it and Nahiry was standing there.

"Jackie, you look like hell," as she brushed her way past me.

"I feel like sludge—warmed over," I reply. "I have a hangover, so please don't talk loudly. My head is pounding."

Nahiry plopped down on the couch. "So, you drank too much Champagne. You must have had a swell time after we left last night." Walking toward the kitchen, "I may have had too much to drink, but I didn't have a swell time last night after everyone left."

"What do you mean by that?"

I came back to sit at the other end of the couch, after getting some aspirin for my head and a ginger-ale for my stomach.

"He tried nothing funny, did he?"

"No, no. He would do nothing like that." I saw the relief in Nahiry's expression.

"After everyone left last night, we went for a walk in his garden. John asked me why I didn't have a man in my life. I told him a short story and then he asked me why I accepted the invitation to go out with him. I then explained to him I had no reason not to trust him because he wasn't interested in me."

Nahiry sat back on the couch. "And what did he say?"

"He told me he was interested in me, and then he kissed me."

"Wow, that's great, Jackie. So, will you see more of each other?"

"Nahiry, I know I enjoyed kissing him very much, but I pulled away from him and left."

Nahiry sat close to the edge of the couch now. "Why Jackie? John and I think you would make a wonderful couple. What happened?"

"Nahiry, I freaked out, I panicked, and old memories of my past hurt came to the surface. When he kissed me, I almost melted in his arms. We felt the attraction we had for each other. When I closed my eyes to let go of my past, I saw my father's face. I couldn't explain to him why I had to leave. I told him I would explain later, but not then. The very thing I've wanted for forever was there and my anxieties surfaced, and I didn't know how to handle it."

"Jacqueline, you had the perfect man for you right in your hands, and you let him get away."

"There's nothing I can do about it now. I don't want to talk about it anymore."

Nahiry studied me, for I don't know how long. "Jackie, do you have feelings for John in any way? If what you felt was real, are you willing to fight for it?"

Tears ran down my face. "I don't know," I admitted.

Nahiry walks toward the door. "Jackie, if you don't know the answers, then I will leave now so you can think about it. I want you to think long and hard, because I don't want to see my best friend, my sister, pass up on love. A love that you deserve. A man that you deserve." As soon as she closed the door, I staggered to my bed and slept the day and night away.

Chapter 8

Finding My Way

HEADING INTO THE OFFICE, I was back to normal as my chipper—depressed self.

"Good morning, Cynthia."

"Hi, Jacqueline." Whispering, "Dr. Simmons is in a bad mood."

"Do you have any clue why?"

"Do you remember the little girl that moved to Washington?"

"Who? Amy?"

"Yes, that's her."

"What about her?"

"He received her test results back from the lab on her blood work. He found out she has leukemia."

The shock from hearing the news made my body feel worse than it already did.

"Dr. Simmons called her parents, and they will be here at one o'clock. He's hurting."

Pounding my hand on the desktop. I couldn't think of anything to say, but I knew how he was feeling.

"Thank you, Cynthia, for telling me."

"Are you all right?"

"I'm fine."

Walking away without making a sound, I opened the door to my office to put my things away. I wasn't fine. I sat contemplating whether I should go into his office. Would he bring up what happened at the party Saturday night? I didn't want to discuss it, but I had to talk to him about Amy, and that was important enough for me to face him.

I knock at his door. It didn't matter who it was. He told them to come in. When I walked in, he looked up from his desk and did a double take when he saw me standing there. My legs trembled. I sat in the chair. "Yes, can I help you?" His voice was icy. He continued to look at the papers on his desk. "Are those Amy's charts?" He didn't answer. "I'm sorry to hear about Amy. I know she's one of your favorite patients." The room fills with total silence. "I came to see if you were all right and if you needed anything?"

Getting up from his chair, he came around to the front of his desk. He looked down at me as though he could see the little girl in me, the broken me from long ago. He then walked over to the window where he could see the view of the city, with cloud-filled skies and bumper-to-bumper traffic.

"You don't have to worry about me. I'll be fine. I can handle this. It's not like I've never had a patient ill before."

"But you've never had a patient you were so close to or cared for, as you do, Amy." His stare was mean, but as soon as it came, it left.

At that moment, I realized I knew him. I knew his heart.

***

I took her words to heart and figured she was right. My body relaxed. "Just so you know, I care about all my patients. If this were one of the other kids, I would feel the same."

"I know. Is there anything we can do for her?"

"I'm not sure. Her Leukemia is aggressive. Much more aggressive than I have ever seen before. We can try to put it in remission, but it might not work. And if it works, we don't know how long it will stay in remission. I would like to be alone now if you don't mind."

"I don't mind. I'll let you know when Amy's parents get here."

"Thank you."

~

I left his office and walked over to Cynthia's desk. "Cynthia, can you call me first when Amy's parents get here?"

"Is Dr. Simmons, okay?"

"He's hurting. This is the first time I've seen him react this way to one of his patients. He cares for Amy. He delivered her, and she's been his patient since birth."

John had Cynthia call most of the patients to reschedule their appointments. Those that couldn't reschedule just saw me for shots or a routine physical.

***

There was another knock at my door. "Yes, come in." I said.

"Dr. Simmons, it's twelve. Would you like something to eat?" Cynthia asks. "No, thank you. Although, if you don't mind, I would like some tea, please."

I knew how to break the news to Amy's parents. It had never been this hard before, and I wished there were the right words to say to any parent about their child. I remember when my mother died. When they came to tell me, I was heartbroken, but this was a little child — one he could help, but possibly not save.

~

As I walked out of my office, "Jacqueline, the Harrisons are here." Cynthia says. I walked over to them. "Nice to see you again. Can you sit for a minute? I'll tell Dr. Simmons you're here."

I glanced at Cynthia to get me some tissues as I walk to his office. I knock softly and open the door. "Dr. Simmons, Amy's parents are here." He was still contemplating the talk. My feelings grew deeper for him as I saw his pain and anguish. Wishing I could comfort him and hold him in my arms. "Would you like for me to be in here when you tell them?"

He cleared his throat before speaking. "Yes, I would like that, if you don't mind?"

"No, I don't mind. I'm glad to help. I'll bring them in. Is that all right?"

"Yes. I guess I can't wait any longer."

I brought Amy's parents in. John looked serious. "Please, sit, Mr. and Mrs. Harrison."

"Thank you," they both expressed.

The talk went as expected, and if it weren't for his profound professionalism, John would have cried and broken down himself. He knew he did his job with the utmost sincerity, and there was nothing else to say. John walks out of his office and into mine, giving the Harrison some time together. I followed behind him.

"God, that was hard. I can't believe this is happening to that little girl." He says.

I step close to him—hesitant. "If it's any conciliation, you did a wonderful job. You explained everything and what they should expect."

"But she's only six-years-old, Jackie. She may not even live to see her thirteenth birthday. Maybe not even her seventh, if we can't get this into remission."

I reacted naturally without realizing and put my arms around him. This was the last piece of the puzzle. I loved him and wasn't afraid he wasn't perfect.

I knew he wasn't my father. I wanted to tell him so, but I couldn't. This was not the right time or place.

He cleared his stuffy nose. "I'm going back in to see if they have questions. Can you make an appointment for Amy? We will need her to see a specialist right away."

"Of course, but can I ask you a question?"

"Sure, what is it?"

"I know they were moving to Washington. What happened?"

"Mr. Harrison's company postponed the move until this year. They were to leave after Christmas. I wouldn't have known anything about it if they hadn't stayed. They brought her into the emergency room a couple of weeks ago, as she was lethargic and they drew the blood work. They wanted to go through all the procedures in the blood tests. So, when they came back with the results yesterday, they called me at home early yesterday morning."

I stare at the pictures on my wall. "As they say, things happen for a reason. Those reasons are unknown to us until we go through them, or we may never know at all. But there is one thing I know for sure. Amy is a strong-willed six-year-old, and believe me, she will fight this every step of the way."

John walks to the door, and with a faint smile, says, "I hope so."

Although I knew I loved him, I couldn't show my feelings at the office. I had to see him somewhere alone. Eager to tell him, I felt like I wanted to explode.

Once home, I had to get my nerves in order, my feelings in order, and the perfect words to say. I didn't want to say the wrong things and push him away. I needed to have the confidence that he would understand why I had to leave him the other night.

~

Later that evening, I drove to his house. No music was playing, and my fingers were around the steering wheel so tight that when I loosened them, they ached. I didn't remember how to get to John's house, so I asked Robert for the address. I pull into the driveway, remembering the crystal white flowing fountain and the smell of the garden. His car was in the driveway. I assumed he had been home for a while. My tongue sticking to the roof of my mouth, I was here to say what I needed to say and wait for his reply. I walked up the three stone steps and rang the chimes. I judged by his expression that he was surprised.

"Hello, John."

***

Although it was lovely to see her beautiful face again, I wondered why she was here. "Hello, Jacqueline, come in." She steps in and stops on a dime to wait for me to close the door. Before I could say anything, she spoke, "I need to talk to you. It's about what happened Saturday." Her words were urgent, but relaxed. I was sure she was there to tell me that what happened between us was all a mistake. "All right, let's go into the garden to be in private." As we walk through the double doors, she rings her hands together. I could see she was trembling.

"Jacqueline, what's wrong? Why are you shaking? Whatever it is, we will get through it."

"First, I came to apologize for leaving the other night without explaining to you why I pulled away." She hesitated and then went on. "Please understand that I enjoyed our evening immensely — and our kiss even more. Something happened when I was about to give in to the passion I felt. At that moment, I saw my father's face. I saw all the imperfections of a man who I loved but couldn't love me in return. Not the way I loved him. I'm not saying I could see my father in you, but I could have been with any man and seen my father standing there staring at me — disapproving of everything I am. To put it bluntly, I got scared at the reality of falling in love with someone who I didn't know could love me back. I admire you as a person, as a doctor, and as a man who loves what he does for children."

There was that word again. For the life of me, I couldn't understand why she admired me so much. "That night, you asked me why I didn't have a man in my life. Deep down, I wanted you to be that man in my life, but I didn't want to go beyond a professional relationship with you, and by doing so, I fell more in love with you each time you were around those kids. I didn't want to spoil our working relationship with my hang-ups. Especially seeing all the women you've dated. You had all the qualities I wanted, but I thought to myself, he can't commit to any one woman. My perception saw you as flawed. The perfect man you weren't. I was looking at the surface and not the man underneath. Even though I want a man in my life, I didn't want to seem desperate." She walks over to the red roses and took a deep, relaxing breath. "I never wanted to know the man underneath. I figured if I kept all those other women in mind, I didn't have to think about you in any other way. Today, I saw a vulnerability. I saw you." Quiet the whole time. I knew it was now time to speak, to shed her fears away. To know what they are and to reassure her I was nothing to fear, because what I've wanted all this time was here. "Well, to be honest, all that changed when you told me about your parents. You had never shared your past with me before, and you finally broke the silence. I understood who you were underneath the smile you present every day. I too, saw you in a different light."

I turned to him. "It terrified me after I told you about my past. Things had to go back to normal. I had to get a grip on my emotions."

"So, how do you feel about me now?" I ask.

"I don't see the flaws in you of my past."

~

He grabs and kisses me with all the love and passion a man who understood what true love could give. We laugh and talk and express the love we shared. Ecstasy was about to ravage their bodies, but he pulls away from me. "I love you, Jacqueline, and I want to be with you." He hesitates and continues. "I know we have never talked about faith and God, but I don't want to make the same mistakes I've made in the past. I want our union to be right before God, and to do that, we must talk about this truthfully and honestly. Right now, I want to make love to you, but I want God to be the head of our love. I grew up in synagogue, and my mother always said to keep God first. When I became a doctor, it never changed my thoughts about faith and God. I just didn't practice faith much, but my mom gave me a firm foundation. *'Train up a child in the way they should go, and they will not depart from it.'* I want us to make sure the foundation for our love together is solid."

His words were astonishing and even a little scary. I had to explain my experiences of prayer. "When I got home from leaving you the other night, I prayed to God for only the second time in my life. I didn't know God existed until I prayed and talk to Him about me. Cynthia is the one who has been talking to me about Jesus so, I could understand. She always tells me God looks at our hearts and sees where the emptiness is, and He's willing to fill it with His love. All we must do is accept it. I want God's love to fill my heart so I can love you with it unbroken. So, are we going to do this together? Accept Jesus into our hearts, so we can love each other?"

"Absolutely, and I want us to do it this coming Sunday," John says.

"So, you can become a Messianic Jewish follower of Christ. After speaking to Cynthia, I started researching and reading the Holy Scriptures. It's still a little confusing, but I read about them."

I didn't know what I was doing, but I knew this was right, and now I could be free of my past.

~

That following Sunday, we accepted Christ as our Lord and Savior. Two people are as happy as newborn babes. We spent so much time together. One day, John walks over to a picture on the wall. Behind it was a safe. He opens it, takes out a box, and walks back to the couch. He sat beside me.

"Jackie, I know I am in love with you—and have been for an awfully long time. In fact, I love you and there's nothing anyone can say to change that."

"I love you too, John."

"This is an heirloom from my family. Passed down from generation to generation. The last person to have it was my mother. She had no daughters, and I was an only child, and so it went to me. Before my mother died, she made me promise to give this to the woman I would marry and spend the rest of my life with. She knew she wouldn't be here long, even though I didn't know it. I promised her I would. Jacqueline, I'm asking you to marry me and spend the rest of our lives together." Opening the box. The ring comprised pure white gold and the most beautiful diamonds.

"Jackie, will you marry me?"

"Yes, John, I will marry you, all of you." He removes the ring from its box.

***

I kissed her with happiness and joy, and then she ran over to the window. "I'm going to be Mrs. John Simmons!" she shouts. The gardener outside cheered.

She ran back and jumped on me. "Dr. John Simmons, I will marry you any day or any time."

"So how about a June Wedding, and then we can take at least a three-week honeymoon. We deserve a vacation." She just stared at her ring. "That's wonderful. Oh, my goodness, I should call Nahiry. I wonder if she called the house yet. Oh, no! I have to call Nana."

I pull her to the couch. "Honey, slow down. You have plenty of time."

"I must confess, Dr. Simmons. I'm glad you were the one for me. Someone I love, not just some random man — and I will cherish this always."

"Well, I must confess something to you as well."

I could see he was serious, but it was more questioning than anything. "What?"

"I never slept with any of those women I dated. I've only had relations with one woman, and it was a long relationship — that's one reason I never got serious with them. After they figured, I would not ask them to my bed. They smothered me, they thought I was gay, or they assumed I didn't find them attractive. Although, I can say I have been in love once."

"Who was she?"

"It's not a way, but is. You're the only woman I've ever been in love with — except maybe my elementary school teacher. But I have never felt like this with anyone else in my life."

Our lives were complete, but one little girl was still in our hearts. "Even with all the joy, I still ache in my heart."

~

I loved him, so I hated to see him hurting, but I understood his pain. "I know Amy is on your mind. All we can do is a help in any way we can and pray to God, she will make it through. We will encourage her parents as much as possible, so they can be strong for her. I had somebody strong in my life when I was growing up."

"Who?"

"Nahiry. She was always there for me and vice versa. I shared all my secrets. Ones I couldn't talk about with anyone else. There was no God to talk to in my life. He never existed in my family. I was the dorky kid on the block, and she didn't turn me away. She has always been more like a sister than a best friend. But now I have two people I can share my secrets with.

John startled me, jumping up quickly. "Oh my, I have to make sure I call my dad first. He'll be upset If I don't tell him beforehand that I'm getting married."

Chapter 9

Nuptials

THE WEDDING OF THE YEAR had arrived. The colors were all amethyst and white. Nahiry was Maid-of-Honor, and why not? His namesake was the Best Man. The wedding march was playing, and Jacqueline was coming down the aisle. Her uncle could give her away.

~

At the reception, "This is John—my best man for those who do not know him. He and his lovely fiancé Nahiry, Jacqueline's best friend, will make the toast this evening. Before I hand it over to him, I want to say to you both, thank you for being there for us every step of the way. Now I hand it over to my best man—and someone who's become a special friend. My namesake, John."

We danced and Krenzl'd around Nana, seated in the middle of the dance floor, crowned with flowers. The party went on until two o'clock in the morning.

~

After the reception, we head to his home. He carried me over the threshold and to his room. "I'm still a little afraid."

"Don't be. I won't betray your love."

"Confession time. I've been with only one man — when I was twenty-one. I haven't since."

"I love you too much to hurt you." Their bodies met as their heat rose. "I need you now." Our mouths glistened, reaching ultimate pleasure. We both formed to each other's body. Our love was one. "Thank you for letting me love you without fear," he says softly. "Mrs. Simmons."

"Yes."

"I never want to let you go."

"I don't want you to let me go, either."

The next morning, the sun glowed through the blinds, and they woke up in each other's arms.

"Good morning, Dr. Simmons."

"Good morning, Mrs. RN, Simmons."

We had found each other, and love had found us.

"Oh my God! No, John. In all the excitement, I forgot to tell you." Panic set in.

"What? What is it?"

"We didn't use any protection. I haven't in nine years!"

He kissed me on the forehead. "Don't worry about it. I love you now, and I'll love you with a child. If you get pregnant right away, then it was by God's design. I want about ten anyway, so this is an effective way to start. With all the love possible." We both laugh. "Well, I don't think we need to rush anything. You know you won't know if you're pregnant for another six weeks from now. So, let's take this one step at a time and try not to mention this again—or to anyone else," he says.

"You know, you're so funny. And what do you mean by ten kids? You're kidding, right? I can't have ten kids. We have to decide right here and now how many children we will have."

He put his hand over my mouth. "I want as many as you want. I can only fertilize the egg. You decide what your limit is. If you decide you only want one child, I will live with that. If you want twenty, I'll live with that as well. I hate to say this, but you're the one who will go through the pain of childbirth. So, you decide. All I ask is that you decide after the first child. I would rather have more than one, but like I said, it's up to you."

"Now I know why I couldn't resist you. My father was so staunch, he showed no emotion. Not that I'm saying that about you. I know you were angry with me. I could tell how you spoke when I knocked on your door. But you didn't let that interfere with what you needed to do."

"I'm going to enjoy learning more about you down through the years, Mrs. Simmons."

"Speaking of learning more about me, I know we have time to get to know each other, but there is something I want to tell you about my past that I think you should know. It may not be significant to you, but it was something I have kept in all these years. Nahiry is the only other person who knows. Remember when I told you about the only man, I had relations with when I was twenty-one? I was immature and didn't know who to turn to or where I could go to get help. No one could or would help me, I thought, and I had no one to talk to about this — other than the man I thought I was pregnant by. I didn't want the shame of having a child unmarried, relying on the man I was seeing was stupid. Of course, I went to one of those clinics, because I wanted no one who knew me to see me. Before it happened, I would say to myself that I would never get an abortion. I couldn't do that and live with myself. But like I said, I couldn't handle the shame of having a child out of wedlock. I took the uncomplicated way out, making an appointment without even knowing if I was pregnant or not. He stuck with me through it all, but later, we had a lot of disagreements. I was ashamed of what I had done, and he didn't want the child anyway, so his nonchalant attitude turned my stomach sour. I found out down the line I may not have been pregnant at all, but I'll never know. That guilt has been with me ever since. Some of it has subsided, with time, but I promised myself that if I got a second chance, I would never make that mistake again. I told Nahiry later down the line when I knew my body better."

He came and sat next to me. "I understand. Although I don't condone abortions and wouldn't perform one, women may now do what they want with their bodies without social shame or consequence. I appreciate you telling me this. Trusting me with your darkest secret. Some women wouldn't. They keep it to themselves until it eats up their insides. I've seen women go insane from the guilt. It's enough you can come to terms with it and not let it get you down. We've learned God is a forgiving God, and I am sure He has forgiven you, but you must forgive yourself. You can't allow this one sin to keep you from moving forward in our relationship with God. We must make sure we are obedient to God's word. Not that we won't ever make a mistake, but we have to talk with each other and communicate our feelings and desires to each other and hold each other accountable." He stood up. "How did you find out you may have not been pregnant?"

"That next month, after the abortion, I went to get birth control pills. I only stayed with them for three months because they didn't agree with me. Through the years, about twice a year it happens, I can go without a menstrual cycle. I found out that's normal for me. I've gone to the doctor, and they say nothing is wrong with me. So, I concluded, I may or may not have been pregnant. So, you don't have to worry about me having only one child. I want three."

"I have to say that is a fair number of children, and if there's more, well, the more the merrier."

"You would say that, wouldn't you?"

~

We were leaving for Hawaii later that evening, and everything was in order. Nahiry and John drove us to the airport. "You two have a wonderful time in Hawaii. Take lots of pictures and bring me back souvenirs," Nahiry says.

"Oh, Nahiry, don't forget to check on the house while we're gone, and I appreciate you taking Misty in for us." I had adopted a tan Pitbull puppy from the shelter and didn't want to leave her with a kennel.

"You're welcome. I just hope you know that if she chews on my shoes, I'll have to send her over to John's. Now get on the plane and don't come back until it's time!"

~

Our excursions in Hawaii were heavenly, the beaches were a dream come true, and the Lua's were unbelievable. We didn't want to leave, but we both had to return to work.

"Although I hate to leave, I think I'm getting homesick," John says.

"You are trying to get back there to a certain patient. A seven-year-old little girl, if you didn't get the clue. When I was trying to take a nap, I heard a certain someone on the phone asking about Amy."

"You caught me. I didn't want you to think I wasn't on the honeymoon."

"John, I knew you were very much into the honeymoon — you were more into it than I was. Trust me enough to share your feelings. You can't keep them inside and expect me not to notice. I was ready to call back home myself, but after you called, I didn't bother. Often, I catch myself thinking that it could be one of our future children, and I would want the doctor who's treating our child to be as concerned and try to help in any way they could. But I implore you, as much as you care for Amy, don't take all of this on your shoulders. Don't think if she doesn't make it, you didn't do enough to help her. All you can do is what you've been doing — and praying — and then after that, it's left up to Him upstairs. That's all we can do."

"I understand. Perhaps telling you I called might lead you to believe my body was present, but my mind was elsewhere."

"I want you to know something. I've worked with you for a long time and know more about you than you of me. When you're focused on work versus something else, I notice. My feelings would have been different if I didn't know what being a doctor meant. But I know all the aspects of it, and I recognize when you are down about a patient. I know what it's like to help you deliver someone else's child. So, please don't hold back from me, and I will do the same. I love you, John."

"I love you too."

~

Amy had gotten better, and after 8 months, it seemed like the Leukemia would go into remission. How long it would last, no one knew.

***

Only close friends and family knew about the special surprise. As she walks closer to me, at the baby shower, "Attention, everyone, can I have your attention, please? My beautiful wife and I have an announcement to make." I kiss her. "We have an extra surprise for you. We know you are wondering why she looks like she's nine months already when she's only seven. This is because we are having twins!" Everyone cheered and clapped.

"We also want to ask Nahiry and John if they would be godmother and godfather to the twins. You don't have to answer now. We want you to think about it because it is a lifelong commitment. So, give us an answer before she goes into labor, which could be in the next two to eight weeks." Everyone laughs with a cheer.

"John, I have to go change into something more comfortable. The twins don't like this dress that much."

"Okay, I think I will join you." He yells, "We will be back, everyone. We just need to change."

~

With two weeks to go to Jacqueline's pregnancy. There was no doubt the twins would go full term.

"John, can you come and put my shoes on? I can't see my feet or the shoes."

"Don't you think you should stay home for your last two weeks? It would be better on your feet and your stomach."

"I figured if I could waddle around still, I would not lie down, because I may not get back up again. Do you know I took fifteen minutes to get out of bed last night, and I had to go to the bathroom? I didn't want to wake you because I know you went to sleep late. Plus, I'd feel more at ease to be at the clinic. Otherwise, you are there and I'm here. Just in case these two want to visit us early."

"I understand. Just don't stand up too much. You need plenty of rest these last two weeks. I don't need you tired out before you get into the delivery room. I meant to ask you if you were getting scared."

"Why should I fear? The most successful, handsome, Jewish OB-GYN Pediatric doctor is by my side. I have nothing to worry about." She laid her head on my chest. "Although I am a little scared of the pain. I don't know what to expect. I've seen thousands of women give birth, but I don't know what it feels like. But I want no painkillers. I want it as natural as possible. Promise me."

"I promise," I say, as I walked into the office door without her. "Good morning, Cynthia."

"Hi, Dr. Simmons. Where is Jackie?"

"Oh! She'll be waddling in pretty soon."

"Ooh! Dr. Simmons, that's mean."

"I just used her exact words. In fact, here she comes now."

"Good morning, Cynthia. How are you?" Jackie asks.

"The question is, how are you doing this morning?" Cynthia replies.

She let out a deep breath of relief. "I'm doing well. My Prince Charming here wants me to stay in bed. You know I'd rather be here at the clinic. Honey, take my things to the office. I'm going to stay out here with Cynthia for a minute. Thank you, darling."

"Jackie, Nahiry called. I didn't know if you were coming in or not. But anyway, she told me to ask you if you wanted to fix up the nursery before or after the twins come?"

"You know, that's a good question. We don't know what they are yet, but we've prepared the nursery to suit either boys or girls or both. I had better call her and tell her to wait until they're born. She's more excited than we are."

"I beg to differ. There is a certain doctor in his office who's about to burst. He's bought something special for you and the twins. I can't tell you what it is, though, so don't ask."

"You are cruel, Cynthia, very cruel."

~

One week passed and then two. I was getting worried. I was hoping the doctors wouldn't have to step in. "John, I hope they don't have to induce my labor or call for a C-Section. You know my mother was almost ten months when she had me. They say what happens to your mother will probably happen to you as payback."

"Jacqueline, you know those babies are going to come any day now. So, don't worry about something that may not even happen. Now, go to sleep and get some rest."

Three hours later, I woke again. "Oh boy, I have to go to the bathroom." After coming back from the bathroom, I climbed back into the bed and nudged John.

"John, John."

"Yes, yes. What is it, babe?"

"John, I had a contraction."

"Okay, just push."

"John, wake up, honey. I had a contraction."

"Contraction? What time is it?"

"It's two thirty-seven. I had it at two thirty-six. I haven't had another one yet."

"Is your bag still by the door?"

"Yes, why wouldn't it be?"

"I don't know. Maybe I'm still asleep." A few minutes passed.

"Oh! John here comes another one. That was only eight minutes since the last one."

"I think we better get you to the hospital."

"I think so too."

~

Arriving at the hospital, John put on his doctor's hat. "Hi, Karen. Jackie's ready to go to her birthing room. Her contractions are five minutes apart now, and her water has already broken. Do you know if Dr. Kramer is on duty tonight?"

"Let me check."

"Everything is all right, honey. Just relax and do your breathing until we get you upstairs," he says, trying to keep me calm.

"Yes, he's on rounds right now," Karen reported back.

"Page him and tell him Jackie will be ready in about an hour. I put her at six centimeters. Okay!"

"John don't leave me. I need you. You can't deliver the babies. I need you to help me."

"I will, honey. Dr. Kramer is already here. I want you to relax and breathe."

My face didn't express calmness. So, he leaned over the wheelchair and kiss me. He wheeled me up to the maternity ward and checked me in and took me to my room. It was a pleasant room with a beautiful view.

"It's normal to be nervous. First-time expectant mothers often feel scared. You're going to be a pro. Can I get you any ice chips?"

"No, I just need to push. Can I push now? I'm feeling a lot of pressure to push."

"Just one second, honey, and then you can do all the pushing you want. So far, you're doing great with the pain." John looked up as Dr. Kramer walked in.

"Hi, Phillip. She picked the right night to deliver."

Dr. Kramer smiles. "Hi, John, is she ready?"

"She's at ten centimeters now. All she has to do is push."

Dr. Kramer spoke softly. "Jackie, I want you to concentrate on my voice and listen to what I'm saying. Okay?"

"Okay, Dr. Kramer."

"On your next contraction, I want you to push. Here it comes now. Push, Jackie, push."

"I'm pushing!"

"A few more times and we'll have the twins swimming in blankets."

***

A short while later, Dr. Kramer had some news to announce. "Jacqueline, you have a brand-new baby boy."

John leaned in close and kissed me. "You're doing a great job, mom."

"Oh, I can feel the other one coming," she says, not having time to savor the moment.

This time, it seemed even faster than the first, and Dr. Kramer was encouraging all the way. "Okay, when the contraction is at its full strength, I want you to push one more time for me, Jackie." The contraction came, and Jackie pushed with all her remaining energy. Dr. Kramer smiled. "Jacqueline, you are now the proud mother of a baby girl."

"Yahoo, I've got a boy and a girl! Honey, you were great. You were wonderful." I couldn't stop smiling.

"I feel terrible and excited and happy and tired and scared all at the same time. I'm glad that's over with. Now I can see my feet. I want to see the babies, John." Jackie says.

"You will see them, sweetheart. Right now, in fact."

"Oh! John, they're so beautiful and little. They have your eyes. How much did they weigh?"

"The first one was five pounds and nine ounces, and the second was five pounds and five ounces. You've had two extremely healthy babies."

The love of my life closed her eyes to rest with both laying on her chest.

"I wish my mother was alive to see how beautifully these two little creatures are."

"She sees them, and I'm sure she's smiling." Jacqueline says.

THE END

ABOUT THE AUTHOR

ARNITA R. LEONARD's passion to write started in high school, and in her early twenties, experiencing vivid dreams, she wrote her first short novella, *Amethyst in Love* (Amazon.com, 2019 eBook and Revised, 2025 print). *Detective Brenda Sayers: Mercy Undercover* (Lulu.com, 2025) was the second novel she wrote after wanting to become a police officer. I established Nita Nae's Books — Truthful Imagination in 2015, to feed the imagination of readers. Other dreams followed, which generated books, such as *Unconditional Counsel* (2019, Revised, 2020 & 2025), *Apocalyptic 7: Salvations Cry* (Lulu.com, 2021, Revised, 2025). Seven novels have since followed — *The Ghosts of Slavery's Dance* (Lulu.com, 2025), *Unconditional Counsel Too: Fate Unbroken, Apocalyptic 8: Angels' of Heavens Army, The Container, Opposing Fruit*, Co-authorship for *Embrace the Dawn: To Live Again* with Margo Leonard, my mom, (Amazon.com, 2024), and my final project, *The Heart of an Untold Legacy*, in which my father from 79 to 86 told the history of our family and the secrets held for so long.

For Author interviews:

Email: nitanaes_books@yahoo.com

Website: https://www.nitanaesbooks.com & Join
Today!

Follow Me on IG, Twitter/X, TikTok & Pinterest @
nitanaesbooks or Arnita R. Leonard

NNB Author's P.O.V. BLOG |
https://www.nitanaesbooks.com/blog

NNB YouTube Channel: click here & Subscribe
Today!